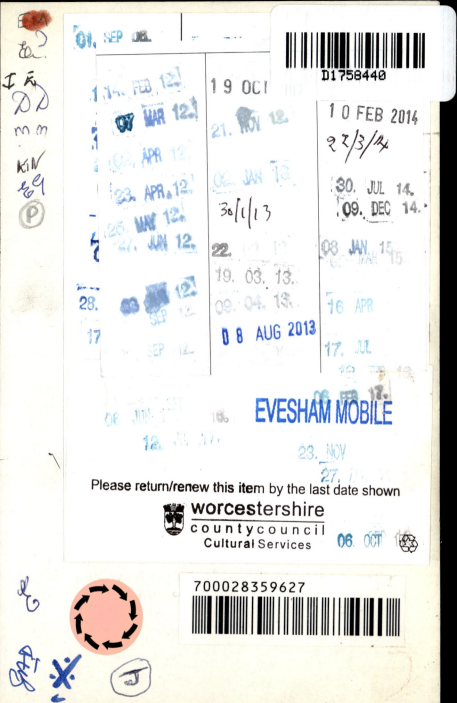

PHOEBE'S CHALLENGE

Phoebe and her younger brother Tom escape from the cotton mills that fate had left them in; and, therefore, from the evil grip of Benjamin Bladderwell . . . Helped by a stranger, they make their way to the north-east coast to trace their mother's family. Little do they realise the dangers yet to befall them, and how important their illusive new friend will become to them if they are to survive the evil that dogs their past.

VALERIE HOLMES

PHOEBE'S CHALLENGE

Complete and Unabridged

LINFORD
Leicester

First published in Great Britain in 2005

First Linford Edition
published 2006

British Library CIP Data

Holmes, Valerie
    Phoebe's challenge.—Large print ed.—
Linford romance library
    1. Love stories
    2. Large type books
    I. Title
    823.9'2 [F]

    ISBN 1–84617–265–9

Published by
F. A. Thorpe (Publishing)
Anstey, Leicestershire

Set by Words & Graphics Ltd.
Anstey, Leicestershire
Printed and bound in Great Britain by
T. J. International Ltd., Padstow, Cornwall

This book is printed on acid-free paper

1

'Thomas Baxter, clear that floor!' Phoebe raised her head in horror as she heard the order bellow out of the miserable mouth of Benjamin Bladderwell, the overseer of the cotton mill.

She saw the fear on her brother's face. He was seven years old and was trying hard to be brave despite being intimidated by the huge figure of a man amidst the terrifying cacophony of the working machines that surrounded them. Bladderwell pointed to the clutter under one of them. 'Move yersel', boy. Now!'

Thomas froze. He was slightly built for his age but, even so, going under a moving machine was a job usually given to the smaller children. She thought this brute of a man sensed Thomas's fear and appeared to relish every minute of it.

Yet, for Thomas's sake she would have to be able to cope with the cruelty of life in the mill until they could make a run for it. He stared blankly as the weaving machines roared and clattered in front of him.

'Move it, yer lazy scum-bag!' Bladderwell took a stride towards Thomas, but the boy had frozen like a statue. They both hated the mill, and that was why they had to escape, before they were weakened by the meagre rations they were fed, or injured by the work and terrible moist and dusty conditions. Phoebe believed in a future where they could both be free again.

As Phoebe stopped her work, placing her basket of wound cotton bobbins on the floor, she ran over to her brother's side. 'I'll do it, Sir. I'm more agile than Thomas and quicker too!' She stood in front of Thomas hoping he would snap out of his fear-filled trance.

She tried to move him aside and, although he was scared, he had not panicked to the point where his blood ran cold and his feet were rooted to the ground. As Phoebe looked at the man's evil sneer, she realised they might have to run for it that very night.

No sooner were Phoebe's words out of her mouth than Bladderwell brought the back of his hand down towards her. She instinctively ducked and the full force of the blow landed across the boy's cheek. Thomas landed hard on the damp floor, scraping his knee through the thin fabric of his clothes. Hatred filled Thomas's eyes.

Somehow they had to escape!

When they were brought to the mill they had worn decent clothes on their backs, but they were exchanged for paupers' rags.

Winded, Thomas tried to stand upright again. He was fighting to recover, breathing in the cotton dust and damp humid air. The factory was kept hot and moist so that the threads did not break on the weaving and spinning machines. No-one seemed to care what happened to the people who had to endure such appalling conditions, so long as the profits were made for the owners. Phoebe believed somewhere there must be a mill that was run in a kinder manner, where people were treated with consideration, but she had not heard of one.

The owner of this mill, James Bartholomew Atkins, grew richer by the day, whilst his workers choked their way through another gruelling day's labour.

Bladderwell cupped her chin in his hand and stared at her before a menacing grin crossed his face. 'Listen, Missy.' He moved his face next to hers. His breath smelled foul and Phoebe tried to pull her face away, but he tightened his grip, until she stopped resisting. 'You can make your life much easier for yoursel' and the sprat. Don't see how he'll survive in here. I'll let the little rat off if you come to the store house now with me and gives Ben a bit of your company.'

Phoebe looked at him bemused. She

was not completely innocent of the way of the world. She had grown up on a farm and knew how the life's cycle worked, and guessed it was much the same for people, but did he really think for one moment she could let him touch her. It was abhorrent to her. 'Never!'

Thomas stood up as Bladderwell threw Phoebe on to the filthy floor to crawl under the machine as it clattered and rattled above her. 'Then get down and crawl in the filth where you belong, and when you've had time to think, missy, yer can crawl back to Benjamin on yer hands and knees!'

Phoebe looked at the back of Bladderwell's jacket as he turned to face the boy. One day soon, I'll make you crawl. I'll see you terrified and cornered, you overgrown bully! She promised her revenge in her mind and, almost at once, as if the man sensed it, Benjamin turned on his heel and picked Thomas up by the scruff of his threadbare wool jacket.

'Ain't you got work to do?' Bladder-well dropped him on the stone floor and reached for his lash. Everyone knew the man was a sadistic brute who enjoyed frightening women and children. Phoebe had to act fast. Her thoughts were filled with hatred as she cowered beneath the great moving monster above her.

There was no room for her to move and clean the mess. She tried to wriggle slowly back out, whilst Bladderwell's attention was elsewhere. Where had the big brave bully been when they needed men to fight Napoleon?

Phoebe forced a picture of her father into her mind — a long ago memory, painful for her to rekindle. A good man like Father had died in the long wars with France, yet a brute like Benjamin Bladderwell still lived. Life was just not fair!

Thomas's anger was too strong for him to hide. There was no point. He was in enough trouble already. His eyes stared accusingly back at the substantial figure bending over him. Phoebe realised they would have to escape today — now. But how?

'I'm goin' to take the skin off your idle little back!' The lines on Bladderwell's face deepened as he gritted his teeth and raised the lash. Thomas curled into the tightest small ball that he could, trying to protect his head.

Phoebe was incensed, she moved quickly in anger without taking enough care. 'Ahhh!' The high shriek of Phoebe's voice stopped the lash from falling.

'Phoebe!' Thomas shouted and ran over to her. She was crying, and lay motionless underneath the great machine. She could neither move forwards nor backwards so great was the fear that had overtaken her. There was an unspoken bond between them and he panicked when he saw blood on her hand.

'Get out of there, you stupid little . . . ' Benjamin Bladderwell's words were drowned out by the noise of

7

the weaving machine, as its clatter grew louder and more irregular. Phoebe had somehow damaged the machine. She couldn't see clearly but she thought something, perhaps part of her sleeve, had caught in it.

Thomas wriggled in behind her. The noise was deafening. Grabbing Phoebe's ankles firmly he tried to gently ease her out. However, he lacked the strength to do it. Suddenly, his own legs were pulled abruptly from behind. The ground seemed to move under him as he was yanked harshly from underneath the machine.

Then Phoebe was unceremoniously dragged out also. Once free, Phoebe could see a gash in her arm that was as long as her middle finger. She swallowed hard and held it to her.

'It will be all right, Phoebe. It's not deep.' Thomas smiled at his sister nervously.

'Oh, Didy.' She tried to smile back. She could see the overseer's face and it both angered and terrified her.

Bladderwell grinned sadistically. Phoebe felt a hatred well up inside her that she had not thought possible to feel in such intensity.

Phoebe and her mother had always called Thomas, Didy. It was short for Didymus, another name used in the bible for Thomas.

Nobody in the factory who was aware of what was happening stopped working to help them. They were all too frightened of losing their precious jobs. Work was hard to come by and although the pay was poor, it was better than the workhouse. The adults would most likely be grateful that it was not their child who had been hurt today. A woman glanced sympathetically at them but did not turn away from her task for fear of punishment.

Thomas helped Phoebe to her feet. 'She needs her wound tending, Sir. That cut should be cleaned and the arm bound.' Thomas's concern for his sister had caused him to forget where he was and that he was already in line for a thorough beating.

His plea fell on deaf ears. Bladderwell had no compassion. He was more concerned about the damaged machine than her plight.

'Get back to your work, girl. You can tie a machine rag around it, then collect up those spindles. Move!' The man snapped out the words. He almost seemed to delight in the terror he spread throughout the mill.

'No!' Thomas was really angry. 'There's cloth everywhere here. She doesn't need to use dirty old pieces. Can't she use a bit of scrap, as nobody else will want it?' Thomas asked angrily.

'It's all right, Didy, I'll manage.' Phoebe, seeing the danger Thomas was already in, tried to act normally, but she was pale and frightened. Her voice had been low, almost like a whisper. It only served to embitter Thomas further. He was headstrong and, although younger than her, he liked to assume the role of her protector.

They had been raised in a fine home,

on a working farm. It had been a new farm, one that had been enclosed and the crops rotated to use the land more effectively. Thomas liked modern thinking. He was not against machines or new ideas, but hated their misuse and the greedy men who abused the new ways.

It was not right that he and Phoebe should have been 'given' to the mill owner to be used as little better than slaves. Yet, they were supposed to feel gratitude for being given this opportunity to work there.

When the lash was raised once more, Thomas reached out and grabbed a besom, which was normally used by the younger children to sweep the floor. He swung it wildly. The lash came down and caught on it, wrapping itself around the handle. Thomas pulled with all his strength and, using the moment of surprise in his favour, managed to jerk it free from Bladderwell's strong hand.

He flipped it off, releasing the broom

once more, and both of them watched in disbelief as it flew through the air. He had expected it to fall to the ground but it didn't. The huge man lurched at him. Phoebe felt her throat tighten in a moment of panic, but the almighty sound of a machine crashing put a halt to the man's intentions, taking his attention away from his prey.

Bladderwell almost fell to his knees as he watched the machine falter, crashing to a halt. Phoebe saw a glint of fear cross his face. Of course, he would be frightened because he was answerable to the mill owner for the upkeep of the machines and their production and maintenance.

The whip landed on one of the weaving machines, becoming tangled in the threads bringing it to a grinding halt. Phoebe gulped. Things had gone too far for them to stay a moment longer.

Benjamin Bladderwell's face that had been bright red, was now slowly turning purple. Thomas held on to the broom.

He pushed Phoebe behind him and grabbed a scrap of fabric from the off-cuts.

'Use this, Phoebe.'

Phoebe took it from him and quickly wrapped it around her arm. Thomas helped to secure it firmly. 'When I say run, run!' she ordered her brother who nodded — there was no choice.

Phoebe started backing towards the large double doors at the end of the mill. Her arm hurt and stung and was bound roughly but it would have to do.

They were near the doorway when Bladderwell ran, storming towards them. Words they had never heard before came rushing out of his mouth. Thomas waited till he was nearly upon them, then jabbed the broom handle hard at the overseer's chin. Bladderwell dodged and the blow glanced off his jawbone. Thomas drew it back, looked the man straight in the eye and grinned. He took great pleasure in deliberately hurling the whole broom into the workings of the nearest machine.

'No!' The roar from Bladderwell's mouth was nearly as loud as the commotion Thomas had caused to the apparatus to make as it crashed to a standstill. The workers ran to the side of the mill in trepidation, in case it would explode. The sound of splintering wood, metal hitting metal and threads snapping, echoed in Thomas and Phoebe's ears amidst the turmoil.

'Run, now, Thomas, for the gates.'

In the yard, men loaded bales on to a horse-drawn wagon, whilst a covered one was taking empty barrels away. They stayed momentarily in the shelter of a brick arch by the river, whilst deciding which was the safest way to go.

'We'll have to cross the river and escape into the woods — quickly!' Thomas ordered. Phoebe knew he was trying not to sound scared. Excitement coursed around her veins as she breathed fresh air again and looked to the trees on the bank opposite.

Phoebe watched the fast-flowing

14

water that had been diverted from its original path to flow under the mill, and power the factory's many machines — all very clever, but never-the-less daunting to her. She had a fear of any mechanical apparatus. Since their father had died, she hated guns and noisy machines. It was as if, to Phoebe, they were a threat that had destroyed the happy family they had been when they lived together on their farm. Only it hadn't been theirs, it was only rented.

Phoebe smiled at Thomas reassuringly, proud of her little brother, but worried for his future. They both leaned forwards to make a run for the bank until two strong hands pulled them firmly back to the seclusion of the archway of the mill gates.

2

Thomas kicked the man's shins, but was grabbed tightly by the neck for his efforts. He reached out for his shirt, but he was being held at arm's length so his attempts to grab him proved fruitless.

Phoebe tried to scream, but a large hand covered her mouth. Thomas shook his head. They wanted to break free, but without attracting any more attention to where they were. If Bladderwell's thugs got hold of them now the beating they'd be given may well be their last.

'Be still!' The voice was firm but quietly spoken. Their captor was over six foot tall, and broad. His dark hair was loosely tied at the neck by a leather thong. Thomas stayed still. Phoebe realised the stranger was also clinging to the shadows. They exchanged glances and both ceased in their struggle. Shouts were heard from behind them in the mill. Benjamin Bladderwell's voice echoed across the yard. 'Find them! Find them — drag them back to me now!'

'Quickly,' the man said firmly. In his strong arms they were lifted on to the back of a wagon full of empty barrels. They were still under the cover of the archway. 'Climb behind them and hide. I'll take you out of the yard.'

Phoebe clambered on to the back of the wagon. Her skirt caught on a nail and ripped. The man stared at her clearly visible calf in the half-light of the archway. Both exchanged embarrassed glances before she scurried behind the barrels to join Thomas.

Before the wagon moved, the sound of running feet could be heard on the cobbled yard. Slowly the wheels turned and it began to move steadily forwards. Brother and sister clung to each other, like statues, not able to move, except for the gentle buffeting of the wagon's motion.

'Did you see 'em?' The voice Phoebe recognised as Seth Barton's, Benjamin's right-hand man — or thug, was asking the wagon driver. Seth Barton was as cruel as Bladderwell, and sneaky too. He seemed to have eyes everywhere. Today, fortunately for Thomas and Phoebe, he had been sent on business in the office or he too would have been in the mill making their escape impossible.

'I thought I heard a splash in the river, but it could've just been the waterwheel I suppose,' their newfound friend lied convincingly, but why should he risk so much to help two strangers? Phoebe had no answers. The wagon moved more swiftly as they left the yard.

'To the river, get the dogs. If the girl's bleedin' they'll find her soon enough.' Seth ran back to the river, cursing them and promising a swift revenge upon the brats for the trouble they had both caused him.

Thomas closed his eyes. Phoebe

looked at him, so young really. Dear God, protect us and guide us. Amen. Her prayer, short and sincere, was replaced in her thoughts by the comforting image of their mother's face. She was filled with a feeling that everything would be all right, if only she kept believing and trusting that it would be. For the first time since they had entered the mill, Phoebe was full of hope.

She closed her eyes tightly and prayed further that they would be taken away from the mill to a place of safety, grateful that they had stayed together.

The wagon's speed increased further as they got on to the valley road. Time seemed endless as the two curled up tightly together, holding on to each other, being jolted and buffeted as the wagon made its way down the old weather-worn roads.

'Will the dogs find us, Phoebe?' Thomas's voice trembled slightly, betraying his consternation.

'Not if they go to the river first. I should think they'll be miles off our scent by now.' Phoebe tried to fill her voice with confidence because she had no idea how strong a dog's sense of smell was. Could they track a scent from a wagon? She decided they couldn't as it was above the ground, unlike a fox or animal that kept mainly to the ground.

When eventually the wagon drew to a halt, they cautiously looked up. 'You can climb out here.'

Their two heads appeared warily over the side. 'Where are we?' Phoebe asked as she peered at the woodland at either side of the road. The forest was dense, letting in little light to its dark undergrowth.

'Who are you and why did you help us?' Thomas asked as he jumped down from the side of the wagon. He was feeling more confident now there was no sign of their pursuers.

The tall figure of the driver appeared from in front of the horses where he had been tethering them to a tree trunk.

Phoebe stared at him. He was strong in stature and features yet his eyes had a gentleness that touched her in a way she could not explain.

'In Blaisdale Woods. I am Matthew. I didn't want to see a young boy and injured girl beaten senseless by an oversized bully — not today anyway. Does that answer your questions?' Matthew smiled broadly at them, but did not wait for an answer. He lifted Phoebe down gently. She was listless and her arm obviously hurt her.

'I am not a girl!' Phoebe protested indignantly.

'Sorry, Ma'am.'

He let her slide down between his two strong hands. She felt the firmness of his grip through the thin cotton of her old dress.

'I apologise. If I may say so, you are in fact a very pretty young woman. My mistake, first impressions can be deceptive.' He nodded politely at

Phoebe and bowed.

Phoebe, who was at a loss for words and confused by her inner reaction to this stranger, flushed slightly and then glanced at Thomas who was screwing his face up in disapproval.

Matthew let out a sigh. 'You will follow.' He pointed to Thomas then, without asking, swept Phoebe up into his arms.

'I can walk unaided!' Phoebe expounded.

'Good. Glad to hear it.' He strode off towards a bush, which he moved to the side with his foot revealing a little-used overgrown path leading into the darkness between the trees.

'Where are you taking us?' Thomas asked.

'To a place that should be safe, at least for a while. That is, if you can keep quiet and don't stray far from it until I tell you to. Put the bush back as it was, Thomas,' the man ordered, but did not look back.

Phoebe felt uncomfortable. She held her arms to her but her unease was caused by not feeling stable in his arms. As if he read her thought he said, 'Phoebe why don't you wrap your arms around my neck?'

'It would hardly be proper.'

Matthew laughed. 'Young lady, none of this is *proper*, but it would make sense and you'd help me to support your weight.'

Phoebe held on to his neck. She relaxed and rested her head against his shoulder.

Thomas released the top of the bramble and it returned naturally to its former position to cover their tracks. 'Won't the wagon give us away?' Thomas asked.

'Boy, if anyone saw it they may wander around or look farther along the road, but I would rather we didn't make it too easy for them to find you. Besides, this is a little-used road and the wagon will be gone soon.'

'How?' Thomas continued.

Matthew stopped and turned whilst still holding Phoebe to him, and peered at Thomas with his deep blue eyes. 'Don't ask too many questions. Too much knowledge can be bad for one so young.' This time the man did not smile. He looked straight into Thomas's eyes. Thomas did not flinch, defiantly he held Matthew's gaze. Slowly, Matthew smiled back and walked on, quickening his step.

Thomas had to slither and slide his way across moist fallen leaves and slippery tree roots that criss-crossed the path's narrow surface. He wished he still had his old boots on. They were strong and warm unlike the ill fitting, worn leather ones he'd been given at the mill.

Thomas looked back at him. 'My father always said if you don't ask you don't find out.'

'Mine told me, what you don't know can't hurt you. Some things you don't need to know, so stop prattling, lad, and follow obediently. I've work to do.'

'What work's that?' Thomas asked, but this time Matthew continued along the path without answering. He looked down at Phoebe's face and shook his head at the boy's persistence. Phoebe could not help but notice a faint scar just below his left ear.

'That must have hurt,' she said.

Matthew looked at her, surprised, not comprehending what she was referring to until she touched it gently with her finger. The fleeting contact caused her a moment of embarrassment and Matthew smiled, colouring slightly.

'That was an old scar from a fight fought many years ago and best forgotten but, alas, I've been blessed with a permanent reminder for my sins.'

'What does it remind you of?' Phoebe asked.

'Not to ask too many questions!' Matthew quickened his pace in silence.

After a while, Matthew told them, 'You'll have to rest up a few days then move on. I'll leave you some bread and victuals tomorrow morning. You'll have to get by as best you can until then.

Don't light a fire or you'll be found.'

'How would we light a fire in these damp woods?' asked Phoebe.

'In a dry hearth, young lady, inside an old cottage.' Matthew smiled down at the pretty woman nestled in his arms.

Phoebe glanced back at Thomas and saw the look of jealousy on his face as he stumbled along behind. He was tired she could tell, cold, hungry and Phoebe felt ashamed that he should suffer whilst she enjoyed the comfort and warmth of Matthew's arms. She had to admit to herself, shamelessly, she had enjoyed them. She'd felt safe and protected for the first time in months. Then she noticed that Thomas's cheek had come up in a bruise where Bladderwell had struck him.

'I can walk, Sir,' Phoebe offered in protest.

'I am so pleased for you. Such things are so easily taken for granted. However, you could not walk at such speed and I am afraid I'm in a hurry due to our little detour.'

They had been walking for a good half-hour when they came across a derelict cottage, overgrown with ivy. It had an old well in front of it and a rusty old plough at one side.

'If you know of this place, how is it no-one else does?' Thomas asked.

'Who said no-one else does, Thomas?' Matthew replied as he stroked a piece of Phoebe's golden hair gently away from her face.

Phoebe felt awkward as she blushed involuntarily. He must think of her as a child. The whole experience was undignified — no matter how pleasing it had felt to her at the time.

Thomas saw her reaction and he looked away in disgust. 'Then won't they look there?' he persisted.

'No, lad. I doubt anyone will be here looking for you.' Matthew disappeared into the cottage with Phoebe.

Thomas looked at the crumbling stone cottage without enthusiasm, then followed them inside. To their surprise, instead of it being barren and empty, it had a small bed against one wall. A new lower roof had been fixed inside the shell of the old damaged one making the cottage cosy and dry inside. In the centre, was an open hearth above which hung a small clean cauldron.

'Is this your home?' Thomas asked as Matthew lay Phoebe down gently on the bed.

'I use it sometimes. Pass me the bottle on the table and the jar of honey from the shelf.'

Thomas brought the two dusty possessions over to the stranger who was now tending his sister's arm. Matthew took the bottle first and with part of the cloth cleaned the cut in her skin. Then he removed the top of the jar and spread a blob of honey over it.

Next he re-wrapped her arm firmly with the unused cloth. 'Leave this alone, don't wet it. I'll return later and make sure you're all right — stay here and please be quiet.' He took a swig from the bottle then offered it to

Phoebe. She drank a little and coughed.

Then Thomas, too, took a swig. He coughed and spluttered as the brandy hit the back of his gullet. 'Brandy!'

Before they could say a word, the tall man left them. Thomas watched him disappear behind a yew tree until his form was lost to the dark. Phoebe was shivering on the cot. Thomas lay down next to her and hugged her closely. It must only have been shortly after mid-day yet, in the depth of this woodland, it could have been midnight.

'You'll be fine, Phoebe,' he told his sister.

She realised it was as much to comfort himself as to offer her any peace of mind.

'Can we trust him?' Thomas asked. 'What if he wants a reward or something? Who is he and what do you think he is?'

Phoebe looked at her brother and she smiled. 'He's our friend — our only one.' She felt so pleased to be outside the mill again.

'Phoebe, he wouldn't have seen to your arm if he wished you ill.'

'No.' The same questions had run through their minds. Matthew's clothes were working clothes, but when Phoebe had held his arm, feeling his shirt, it was a finer quality than her father had ever worn. His boots fitted him, and were well made under the dust and dirt.

'No, you're right,' he said.

She rested her head on his and stroked his hair gently with her good arm. 'He has kind eyes and a handsome face.'

Thomas shook his head and then relaxed into a deep sleep. Phoebe, although decidedly determined to stay alert and on guard, had had so little sleep in the month that they had been at the mill that she too felt very tired.

Phoebe's thoughts returned to her mother, though. She had been taken into the poorhouse when her illness had prevented them from maintaining the farm. No rent, no farm. So they had been given work at the mill to pay for their own and their mother's keep. No sooner had they been established at the mill than they had been told she was dead and that now they had to stay there, permanently.

Phoebe felt restless, she wanted to live near the sea. Somewhere like her mother had at Ebton. She explored the cottage by the light of the small lamp. In the hearth of the fire she saw the edge of some burned parchment. She picked it up to place on to the fire when she saw some writing on it and uncurled it carefully.

Find and follow Le . . . The rest of the message had been burned.

Phoebe wondered whom L was and who had been told to follow and find him. Was it some sort of instruction to Matthew? Whatever it was she put it into the pocket of her dress for safekeeping.

3

'Aghh!' Thomas screamed, as he awoke, Matthew had gently rocked his arm to rouse him.

'It's me, boy. Matthew.' The boy shivered at first, but soon realised that this was a friend, not Bladderwell or anyone from the factory.

Phoebe stirred next to him, rubbing her eyes against the light from the oil lamp that Matthew was holding. Both Phoebe and Thomas shivered because of the chill in the air. Phoebe was only wearing the old cotton girl's dress they had given her in the mill. Thomas at least had a rough woven waistcoat to add a layer of warmth over his shirt.

Matthew placed the lamp carefully on the table and wrapped a large woollen blanket around the two of them. Thomas sniffed it. It was clean and felt fresh. They had been given one at the mill that was itchy and crawled with lice.

'You nearly scared me to death!' Thomas said angrily. 'Do you always creep up on folk when they're sleeping?'

'These are for you.' Matthew dropped down two pairs of worn but good quality trousers, shirts and jackets. Next he pulled out a pair of old woollen hats from his pocket. 'And I came in quietly so as not to startle you!' Matthew grinned. 'Remember, Thomas, this is my lair. I'll creep in, or burst in whenever I please.'

'You do live here, then?' Thomas asked.

'Sometimes,' was the brief reply he received.

Thomas looked through the clothes. 'What about Phoebe?' Thomas asked. 'She's nothing to wear.'

Phoebe thought he did not mean to sound ungrateful, but what use was it if he had a spare set of clothes whilst she had none?

Thomas sat on the floor pulling on

his warmer and better fitting clothes that Matthew had brought to him.

Phoebe noticed the edge of a scar showing under the scarf Matthew was wearing around his neck. 'I meant them to be for the both of you. I apologise that I could not bring clothes more befitting a young lady. But you will notice one set is somewhat larger than the other.' Matthew stood and bowed humbly to them, sweeping low. Although Phoebe knew he was being sarcastic there was flamboyance about the man's movements that betrayed a natural gentility. Who was he? What was he?

'You're no servant, Sir. Who are you?' Thomas asked as he chose the much smaller trousers from the pile and nudged Phoebe to take the others.

Matthew laid out a loaf of bread and some mutton on the table. Thomas ran over to it and took a deep breath of its fresh smell. Phoebe eagerly appeared at his side, her face flushed, and she saw for the first time since they were taken from their home farm that his old sparkle had returned. Her smile was broad, her cheeks were flushed pink with excitement and she also looked happy.

'I've always wanted to be a boy,' she said honestly as she looked up at Matthew. She was warm and covered and felt comfortable and secure. She did not know it but the clothes she wore accentuated her figure and made her look more womanly than the old bedraggled dress had.

'Please don't become one, for many a young man would suffer at the loss of such a beautiful female.' Matthew looked straight into her eyes. She wondered if he were mocking her, yet he did not smile at her.

'Well, Phoebe, you will be able to travel further and more comfortably dressed like that,' Matthew said honestly.

'This meat is freshly cooked,' Phoebe said in delight as she watched Matthew unwrap a piece from a cloth and cut off a portion with his knife.

'Then enjoy it.' He looked at Thomas. 'And don't question anymore. You'll have to be gone before tonight or it'll become too dangerous for you.' Matthew poured out a mug of ale for each of them.

Phoebe drank it gladly but felt her head swim a little because, in her thirsty state, she had gulped it down so quickly.

'Eat some more food, Phoebe,' Matthew said, and grinned at her rosy cheeks.

'Couldn't we hide here for a while, just until the fuss dies down,' Thomas asked, looking at the last crumbs on the table and feeling the fullness in his belly.

Phoebe could not remember how long it had been since they had eaten so well. The bread at the mill had been stale, meat non-existent or inedible and the water icy cold — at least it came from the fresh water well.

'I'm sorry, lad. You have to go

tonight, but I'll see to your sister's arm before you go, and give you some food to take you on your way.' The stranger stood up and moved towards the shelves where he kept the jar of honey.

'Where are we to go?' Phoebe's voice caused him to look back.

She thought she saw a look of concern in his eyes but he seemed to be ill at ease, as if in two minds as to what to do about it.

Thomas thought he saw Matthew's face soften in a way that he had not shown before, even though he had been kind to them so far.

'Thomas, where had you planned to go?' Matthew turned the honey jar slowly and thoughtfully in his hand.

Thomas shifted uneasily. 'Phoebe?'

Neither wanted to appear foolish. They had done something rash and both knew they had nowhere to run. 'Along the road to Hangman's Gill then down to the coast.' Phoebe felt pleased with herself, as she had managed to sound confident. At least she now had a plan. In her mind she knew it was right as it fitted in with a story their mother had told her years ago. They would go to the sea.

Matthew's face changed immediately. 'You can't, not there — not tonight. It would be far too dangerous. You must take the north road. Hangman's Gill is no place for innocents!' Matthew's face had hardened. 'Take the north road until you get to the bridge that crosses the big river. Then follow the big river towards the coast road. Half a mile down there is a chapel. Wait there until daybreak when I'll collect you.

'Listen, if you have any sense in your head take my advice. Stay out of the Gill this night and await my arrival in the morning. We'll sort out your dilemma tomorrow.'

'Why should we?' Thomas snapped back.

'Because, boy, I am giving you some damn good advice. Take it!'

Phoebe watched as Matthew tore her old dress into strips. As the material ripped, she thought Matthew looked either very angry or concerned. He obviously felt he could not abandon them, yet did not relish having the extra burden.

'Here,' Matthew called to Phoebe. Matthew was a total stranger to her yet her intuition told her to trust him. He was a mystery and a challenge, both of which Phoebe found attractive.

Thomas watched him closely as he redressed and bound her arm. She could sense her brother's unease at the closeness and familiarity between her and Matthew as he saw to her cut.

Phoebe's head reeled with unanswered questions. Who was he? What was he? Why had he helped them? He was well spoken and had found them decent clothes and fine food. But something wasn't right about him. He was a man of mystery, and Phoebe was bemused by him.

Phoebe looked at Thomas. He liked solving problems too. In the short time he had been at the mill he had figured out how the force of the water moved the turbines that powered the machines. To Thomas they were as fascinating as Phoebe had found them frightening. She was more concerned with the plight of the many women and children who spent their lives working long hours, until they were so tired they inevitably had accidents, or worse, were killed.

'Go soon, take the food that is left and make it last till I find you. If I don't then God alone knows where your next meal will come from after this one. If you make good speed you will reach the estuary by nightfall. Then tomorrow I'll take you to the coast if you still want to go there. Do you have family there?'

Matthew showed a concern for them that obviously touched Phoebe, but she could not understand why. If he were so bothered about their future, wouldn't he let them stay with him? Under the circumstances the usual rules of decorum just didn't apply.

'Yes,' Thomas lied.

'Then God speed.' Matthew looked at Phoebe's face, she had shot Thomas an angry look. Why had he lied?

'Take care, both of you. Be gone before I return. These are dangerous parts,' Matthew warned them, then swiftly left.

'Matthew!' Phoebe called after him.

The man turned to face her. 'What is it?'

'Thank you,' she shouted back.

Matthew smiled at her, warmly and genuinely. 'I would dearly like to say, it's my pleasure.' He waved to them before walking past the well, making the sign of the cross on his chest as he passed by.

'He always does that,' Phoebe said and looked at her brother. 'When we came here yesterday he crossed himself as he went around the well.'

Thomas shivered uneasily.

'Thomas, you fill the leather bottle with water from the well and I'll wrap up the rest of the meat in my old dress. Do you think he would mind if we took

the jar of honey too? Thomas . . . '
Phoebe looked at him and he had
turned quite pale as he stood holding
the empty bottle. 'Thomas, are you all
right?' Phoebe raised her voice.

'Should we both go . . . to the well?'
Thomas sounded quite serious. 'If a
grown man crossed himself there, then
I do not want to go on my own. I saw
something moving near it last night.
Phoebe, I'm not frightened or anything.
It's just I don't think we should
separate. He did say these are dangerous parts. Yes, we'd best stick together.'

Phoebe could see that Thomas felt
better already because he had justified
his hesitancy. He picked up the bundle
of cloth that Phoebe had prepared and
walked towards the door. 'Phoebe, let's
take the knife and blanket too.'

Phoebe decided that as they were
already wanted for wrecking machines,
petty theft, if that was what Matthew
decided to call it, was the least of their
troubles.

She folded the blanket in half and

wrapped it around her like a shawl. When they stepped out into the cold air she was grateful for it. The knife she placed carefully inside the bundle.

Both walked cautiously over to the well. The brick around it was covered in ivy. Thomas's feet had stopped, but Phoebe walked up to it. She stretched out her hand and slowly guided the bucket down until it touched the water below. As she carefully hauled it back up, she heard Thomas say, 'Hurry, let's go!'

They both ran towards the road. Phoebe thought it was going to be a long night, but the thought that Matthew was to return to her — them, in the morning warmed her heart and lifted her spirits.

4

'Didy, isn't this the north?' Phoebe pointed to the road to her left, where their track met the big coach road joining York and Newcastle. It had been much improved by the turnpike roads.

Tolls were now charged for people to use them. The new methods of road building introduced by Thomas Telford and John Macadam had increased the speed of coach travel tremendously. Phoebe dreamed of one day travelling in a large coach to York or even London.

'Yes,' Thomas replied, but cut straight across it to the old pot-holed track, which Phoebe's intuition told her must lead them to the coast.

'Matthew told us to take this one and wait for him in the old chapel by the big river,' Phoebe persisted.

'Yes, I know he did, but who says we

have to do what he says? We don't even know who he is, Phoebe.' Thomas came back for her, took hold of her hand and guided her across safely.

'He's helped us, and besides Thomas, we don't have any relatives near the coast, do we?' Phoebe wrapped the blanket more firmly around her as she stared along the dark and lonely track.

'No — well, I doubt it. Mother once told me she came from over Ebton way.' Thomas shrugged. 'But I know that it's where we must go, because if we have any folk at all of our own then that's where they'll be.'

Phoebe sighed. 'I'm the eldest. I should make the decision, Thomas. Can we really base such a decision on a whim?' She stopped, tugged his arm until he faced her, and stared at him.

'Phoebe, I'm a man and you're a girl. Therefore I decide. That is the way the world is. Besides, it isn't just a whim!'

'Correction, Thomas Elgie, you are a boy and I'm a woman!' Phoebe replied angrily. She clenched her fists and raised her nose slightly. 'I had a nightmare last night about machines trying to eat me up and I'll go where help can take me as far away from them as possible!'

'You had a nightmare based on your fear. A machine is a machine. It has no mind of its own and can't eat anyone up. It's stupid, thoughtless bullies like Bladderwell who make them dangerous. And you look like a mighty funny woman dressed like that anyway. Don't let those breeches fool you, you're still a female and, as such, it is up to your father, brother or husband to look after you. The law says so!' Thomas raised his voice to strengthen his point.

'Well the law's wrong! Mary Wollstonecroft knew so. Mother taught me how to read by the bible and Mary's books. She spoke out for women and their rights. The law also says you shouldn't wreck other people's machines, but that didn't stop you, did it, Didy?' Phoebe made her point.

'I was trying to protect you! Pa never

liked you and Mother reading things like that.' Thomas paused for a moment. Both knew it was rare that Thomas could remember something about his father. He had been trying so hard the last few weeks to recall anything of him, and it had only brought him feelings of emptiness and pain. 'He said it would get you into too much trouble with folk. He was right. People don't want to hear women speaking like men.'

They were cold, frightened and hungry and the last thing they needed was to have a fight. Usually they got on really well, but fate had put them into a totally unknown and daunting situation. Phoebe realised they had to stick together.

'Besides, you only want to go to the chapel to meet with Matthew. You're soft on him, shame on you Phoebe Elgie.'

'I am not, Thomas,' Phoebe denied what she knew to be the truth. She was angry with herself more than Thomas.

She could make no sense of the way she felt at all, but with all her heart she wanted to see him again. He was her challenge and she wanted to know everything about him.

'So tell me who and what he is? Why trust a stranger just because he talks sweet to you and had a strong body?' Thomas gritted his teeth as he stared at Phoebe.

'I'm sorry, Didy. I know it seems unfair and you — well, we are both scared and life is so unfair. I trust Matthew, and I can think and speak out as well as any man. My body is not as strong, but I don't want to marry unless a man can respect me for the person I really am.' Phoebe put an arm across his shoulders, wrapping the blanket around the two of them. 'Let's be friends again,' Phoebe said softly.

Just then they heard the sound of two riders approaching. They ran into the forest and hid. The riders were travelling north.

'Bladderwell!' Thomas whispered.

'Are you sure?' Phoebe asked.

'Yes,' Thomas replied, but Phoebe did not know for sure if he were telling the truth. 'We best go to the coast now. They've got the river covered.'

Phoebe nodded her agreement, not sure if she were being gulled by Thomas, but tired of the fight. She prayed that if it were meant, Matthew would cross their path again, and soon.

Grateful for the warmth and closeness, Thomas smirked back at her. 'I know you can be clever, Phoebe, and so did Pa, from what Mother said of him. The thing is, it will take a long time to change the way that people think now.' She squeezed him close as they walked along. 'It will be really dark soon, Phoebe. I know that the gill is off this road somewhere. I think Mother told me once. If we follow it down, we shall get to the coast near Stangcliffe, just south of Ebton. Beyond that I don't know. Just think, Phoebe, if we could hear gulls and smell salt in the air, how marvellous it will be. No more dust.'

Thomas looked around him. Phoebe could see trees in the dark dim distance.

'Mother once lived in a big manor house. I think she was a maid or something. Sunnington Hall was its name. Who knows, they may even offer us work? At least we will in some way be nearer to her again,' Phoebe added as if to offer comfort to him.

'Then I say we should follow the coastal path,' Thomas said. 'Agreed?'

'Agreed,' Phoebe said reluctantly.

★ ★ ★

For the next hour they kept walking until they reached a point where the road narrowed between two halves of a forest. It was pitch black and the strange haunting sounds that came from animals hidden by the shadows succeeded in scaring them both. The slight smell of salt in the air told them, reassuringly, they were nearing the sea.

'What was that?' Thomas stopped.

Crack. A noise was heard from the depths of the forest.

'Quick, Phoebe, hide!' They both ran into a thick bush surrounded by fern just inside the forest. For a few moments all was quiet. Then a faint glimmer of a light appeared through the trees. It swayed three times as if giving a signal — then went out.

Phoebe held her breath for what seemed like an age to her. Both breathed slowly as if the slightest movement would betray them.

Silently, figures emerged from the forest around them. Then a cart appeared along the track. It was strangely quiet as the horse's hooves were covered in sackcloth. All the figures wore hoods or hats and had dark cloths wrapped around their faces. It would be impossible for them to identify anyone even if they saw them.

'Is it a press gang?' Thomas asked by mouthing the words almost silently into Phoebe's ear. Press gangs were feared the breadth of the country. Phoebe turned her head so that she could speak straight into Thomas's ear.

'I don't think so. They'd march their victims along the road. They usually grab people from the towns.' Press gangs were like authorised kidnappers. They would enlist boys and men for His Majesty's Navy to fight in the wars against France. The sudden loss of a husband or son could put the family that was left in poverty, but the demand for men to man the Navy's ships was considered to be more important.

Slowly and cautiously, figures emerged from the gill carrying barrels and bales of cloth — most likely silk. Phoebe realised they were carrying contraband goods.

'Smugglers!' she said under her breath. Government taxes were so high that these so-called 'free-traders' smuggled goods into the country. The rewards were high but the risks they took were great. If caught, they could be hanged or transported.

In front of them the goods were

loaded silently on to the wagon. Each man hoisted his load up and then, without a word, disappeared back into the forest. Once the wagon was full, the driver went on his way.

Phoebe and Thomas watched until it was out of sight. All around them the woods were alive with the smugglers returning into its depths, when a cry went up.

'Revenue men!' Suddenly the sound of cutlass against cutlass was heard. The preventative services were always trying to clamp down on the illicit smuggling activity. A pistol shot rang out, but missed its target.

Thomas and Phoebe put their heads low, close to the moist ground. Fights were breaking everywhere and the fern and bracken above their heads moved. Phoebe nearly gasped but managed to stifle her cry.

'Levi! Behind you!' ' A shout was heard. Thomas peered through the leaves and saw a tall figure turn and attack an approaching preventative officer. Levi threw a stone hard, knocking the pistol from his opponent's hand before he had a chance to fire his shot. He groaned and staggered backwards only to raise his cutlass and come forward to attack.

'Ahh!' Suddenly the man screamed out and fell to the ground as a batman carrying a blackthorn club struck him from behind.

'You fool! You've killed him.' Levi bent over the body.

'You wants to repeat that do yer?' The giant of a man swung the club, narrowly missing Levi's head.

Levi dived and rolled down the bank to take cover in their hiding place. Thomas was ready to run, but although the eyes that peered from the masked face could not avoid seeing them, it was he who jumped up and ran the opposite way with the tall man in pursuit.

'Why did that monster turn on Levi, when he had saved him from being shot?' Thomas asked Phoebe as they

moved swiftly through the undergrowth.

'Because he accused him of murdering the man,' she replied.

'He did. We saw him too!'

'Yes, Thomas. That's why we must
escape, because we witnessed a murder.
The man with the club would not rest
until we were dead also. Levi should
have just thanked him.'

Phoebe wondered if he, too, were
dead now. The man had not betrayed
their presence, but why? She would
have a lot to thank God for in her
prayers that night.

'Come, Thomas.' Phoebe led the way
down the other side of the gill, keeping
their heads low until they came to an
old oak tree.

'Let's shelter here, Phoebe,' Thomas
said enthusiastically. She thought they
had covered enough ground so they
nestled down against its huge trunk,
stopping to catch their breath. Both
drank greedily from the bottle of water
they were carrying. Phoebe suddenly

felt faint. She had not realised just how thirsty she was.

Thomas closed his eyes fleetingly. 'Yes, we will,' he spoke the words after a few moments of silence.

'We'll what, Didy?'

'Find Levi. He didn't disclose us — we should help him too.'

His hand, still holding the bottle, dropped down, but Phoebe's scream awoke his senses once more as the clang of the iron mantrap snapped viciously shut next to him — snap! His face paled, as he looked down horrified at the sight that greeted him.

5

Phoebe screamed as the great jagged jaws of the mantrap snapped shut as Thomas lowered his arm.

'Didy!' Phoebe grabbed his collar pulling him to her. The bottle was torn to pieces as the trap snatched it — only inches from his own hand. Horrified, they hugged each other closely for a moment as they carefully studied the long grass and the patches of bracken and fern that surrounded them. How many more were there? How near had they come to losing a limb?

'If they've mantraps on this side of the gill we must be on someone's private land.' Phoebe shook her head on disbelief. 'Trespassers we are now. We've seen a murder, run away as wreckers of machines and now this! How is it those smugglers didn't walk into one of them?' she asked naively.

'They obviously knew what to look for,' Thomas said, looking around frantically. 'Or they know who set them,' he added thoughtfully.

'Father never used them. He said that they were too cruel. He'd seen a man lose his foot in one, then his life from poisoning of the blood. He never wanted to do that to anyone on his land.' Phoebe looked down thoughtfully until she heard something moving between the trees ahead of them.' 'What's that?'

'I don't know,' Thomas said, standing up carefully. 'Someone's coming. Look over there, behind that birch tree!' There was no time to think and nowhere to run, not when they now knew the hidden dangers of the forest.

Like scared rabbits they did not move as a man appeared before them holding a pistol and a large cudgel. Phoebe could clearly see the man's face, though, so he was not one of the smugglers.

'Stay there, lest you want a bullet in

yer back!' The man's voice was rough and threatening. His bearded face appeared like a bear beneath his cloth hat. From his waistcoat and breeches he looked to Phoebe like an overseer or gamekeeper. They had definitely wandered on to private land. She now wished they had listened to Matthew's words and headed north.

'We're lost!' Thomas shouted. 'We only wanted the shelter of the tree, but this trap surprised us.' He tried to sound innocent, lost and young, but his words had no effect on the man.

Just like Benjamin Bladderwell, Phoebe thought. Thomas squeezed Phoebe's hand gently. In her breeches and cap she hoped she looked like a youth. Carefully she picked up the blanket, wrapping it around them as if to add substance to what Thomas was saying.

The gamekeeper hooked his cudgel back on his belt. He took a piece of rope from around his waist. 'Come 'ere, both of you and no tricks, you hear me?

You're on Lord Sunnington's estate. You don't belong around these parts and you'll answer to him!' His bearded face showed no expression.

He beckoned them to him, narrowing eyes — glowering at them. Shaking the rope free with his left hand, he cracked it like a whip, and then looped one end around his hand.

As they approached, the brute surprised Thomas by expertly and swiftly looping a makeshift noose around the boy's neck. Thomas was taken completely off-guard. Phoebe had presumed it was going to be used to tie their hands together. Thomas grappled at the rope with his hands as it tightened. The more he wriggled the more it gripped his neck. The man was still pointing his pistol at Phoebe who had run forward to help Thomas. 'Touch him, lass, and you gets it.'

Phoebe hesitated. 'You're choking him.' She watched helplessly as Thomas struggled. The man only laughed at his futile efforts. 'Do you want the murder

of a small boy on your conscience, Sir?'
Phoebe was trying to keep her voice
calm, but there was a tell-tale wobble in
it. She was scared.

'You cheeky young harpy. You'll fetch
a price down the market.'

Anger rose within Phoebe. 'How dare
you insult me. I am not a piece of
chattel that you can buy and sell at
will!' It was not unheard of for women
to be sold at market, so poor were their
rights.

'Wicked tongue, too. I'll be tamin'
that afore I gets yer to the auction. Stop
squirmin', boy, and I'll slacken it.'
Thomas stayed still.

The gamekeeper lifted him to his feet
with one strong hand. The man was still
keeping his eyes firmly on Phoebe and a
tight hold on the rope. 'Now, you're
both comin' with me. If you runs, lass
— he dies. Understand?'

Phoebe nodded and Thomas glared
angrily at the earth beneath his feet.

The gamekeeper made them walk
along the narrow path leading out of

61

the gill on to a broader stony one that skirted a large open field. They adjusted their eyes from the dim darkness of the gill to the bright moonlight, which outlined a large country house in the distance.

It must surely be a palace fit for a king, Phoebe thought, but not for long as Thomas was dragged along the stone-ridden path. He could barely keep from stumbling, as the man took no account of the smaller strides his young legs took or of the imposition of being half choked by a rope around his neck.

Phoebe wondered if he had been a slaver. He showed no compassion for Thomas's suffering and seemed an expert at handling the rope.

It was their mother who had told them about the men that traded in buying and selling people from foreign countries as if they were animals. She believed in the words of a man called William Wilberforce who was trying to have the trade stopped.

'Mornin', Marwood. Pray tell me what game you have caught in the woods so early in the small hours of the morning.' The tall figure, dressed sombrely in a long black jacket and hat sat on a large donkey. He held in his hand what looked to Phoebe like a small book — possibly a bible?

The man with the pistol put it back in his belt and hauled Thomas in front of him. With a firm foot behind his rump, he pushed him hard so that Thomas fell to the ground.

For one moment Phoebe's mind flashed back to Benjamin Bladderwell and the mill floor. Will we never be free of over-sized bullies?

'Word 'ad it, there were smugglers out this night, but these are the only two I've found, Reverend.'

'They don't look much like smugglers to me, Marwood.'

The gamekeeper shrugged and opened his mouth to reply but the Reverend continued, 'I'm glad you're being so diligent in your work, but you should take care. They killed a revenue man over at Becker's Ridge last week.'

'We're not smugglers. We were just lost and sheltered in the woods,' Phoebe said defiantly, as she approached the preacher. However, he put his hand up as if to stop her coming any nearer.

'And what did you see in them woods, lass? Tell us that!' Marwood asked, but Thomas had regained his composure and, before he straightened up, stared at the imposing figure on the mule. There was something about his tall build, his manner and his voice that was so familiar.

Phoebe stepped nearer. 'Please, Sir, we're lost. We did not know we trespassed we . . . ' She looked into the man's face beneath his hat and her words stopped as she realised who he was. Matthew!

Before she had a chance to speak his name, Matthew gave her a warning look from behind the rims of a round pair of spectacles that he was wearing.

Phoebe opened her mouth to continue, honestly, as she had always been taught to. They had been lost.

Thomas said, 'We saw and heard nothing, except for this man who found us resting by a tree.' He pointed to Marwood but did not take his eyes from Matthew.

Both were wondering, what was he? Was he really a preacher man? 'What do you intend to do with them?' Matthew asked. Thomas nudged Phoebe gently as he too had realised who he was.

'I'm takin' 'em up to the big house. The master will know what he wants to do with the likes of them.' Marwood bent to pick up the rope again. He looked annoyed. Phoebe thought that, if Matthew had not discovered them, then the man might well have sold them on unnoticed.

'I shouldn't if I were you, but if you are set on it, then God speed you on your way.' Matthew walked the mule over to the side of the track as if to get out of their way. Phoebe looked imploringly at him, but he just nodded politely and looked away.

'Thank ye.' Marwood pulled Thomas up to his feet and grabbed his rope again. Then, as if Matthew's words had just sunk in, he turned back to him. 'Why wouldn't you?' he asked casually.

'Because your master is expecting a large party of guests, very important guests. They arrive today. They'll be staying for a week as I understand it, Lord and Lady Greesham arrived last night. He will not want any unpleasantness during their visits, will he? I'll speak to him about the matter tomorrow. Good day.' Matthew slowly kicked the mule onwards.

'Then where would you suggest I take them, Reverend?' Marwood asked whilst glaring at Thomas.

Phoebe realised the man's plans had been ruined by Matthew's saying he would speak to the Lord of the Hall about them.

Matthew turned the mule to face them. He removed his hat and scratched his head thoughtfully. 'Give me the rope. I shall take them with me to Ebton. I am sure there, the good Lord will provide gainful employment for them.'

Marwood handed the rope to Matthew, but before releasing it asked, 'What brings your good self out on a night such as this?'

'My work, which is my life, is to be near God. How to be more so than on such a beautiful clear night as this.'

'Aye, well I'm goin' to get a couple of hours' more sleep.' The man turned towards the house then paused momentarily. 'I shouldn't have thought it would make a good night for smugglin', seein' as it is so clear an all.'

'Perhaps that's what the smugglers were hoping people would think.'

6

Matthew dismounted once they were in the cover of the gill. He stood before them tall, dark, imposing yet smiling gently back at them. Phoebe was glad that she already knew this figure in black, because, without his smile, his size would make him look quite daunting.

'What are you doing here? I told you to go north and avoid the wooded gill tonight!' He looked from Phoebe to Thomas and raised a quizzical eyebrow in annoyance. 'Do you not understand plain English?'

Both Thomas and Phoebe stared down at their feet. Neither of them could think of a good reason to give him in the light of their current predicament.

He cupped Phoebe's chin in one of his large hands and tilted her head gently up so he could see her face clearly. She remembered the rough gesture of Bladderwell, when he had tried to proposition her. As she stared into the depth of Matthew's eyes as if trying to read his very soul, she thought these men could not be further apart in character. 'You are very tired. I'll take you both to my cottage, humble as it is, and we will find you some food. We can talk there, in private and warmth.'

Thomas was still staring down at the ground. Angrily, he loosened the rope from around his neck, and threw it at a birch tree.

Phoebe felt humiliated, yet was still determined to follow Thomas's plan to live by the sea in their mother's home town. They had to! It was all they had left to take them into an unknown future. They knew they still had to head for the coast. If that was where the preacher, Matthew, was headed, then perhaps things had worked out for the best.

'May I?' Matthew bent down and

lifted Phoebe on to the mule, wrapping the blanket around her.

She smiled gratefully. 'You may,' she said, as she found her anger dissipated, 'preacher man.'

Phoebe looked into the dark undergrowth. Was the murderer still out with his bloodied club? Should she tell Matthew?

'Many slaves wish they'd had the opportunity to free themselves so easily. You're a fortunate young man, Thomas. You have been freed and you are with a friend, but more than this, you have a white skin. Slaves are trapped in our land in more ways than by chains alone. Remember what that noose felt like and when you grow to be a man, you might be able to change this world for the better.'

Thomas understood what the preacher was saying, but could not see how someone as poor as himself would be able to change anything. 'You certainly know how to preach,' Thomas said quietly.

'I think, Thomas, you are being guided away from danger. Our paths appear destined to cross. Now, may I suggest you ride on the mule with your sister?' Matthew straightened up, but Thomas did not move.

'No! I can walk like you. I'm not a child anymore.' Thomas stared defiantly up at the face that he was now so familiar with, yet had known for just a short time. 'If I am old enough to work in a mill then I am old enough to walk like you.' Thomas spoke boldly, even though his body ached for lack of sleep and his belly groaned again for food.

'Thomas,' Matthew lowered his voice to a whisper, 'Phoebe is near to exhaustion. I need to get her to warmth and food as soon as I can. We will make better progress, my friend, if you both sit on the mule and I lead it down the steepest and shortest cut through the gill. It comes out behind the chapel. I'll need your strong arms to support her as we descend.' Matthew looked imploringly at him.

Phoebe heard the preacher man's words and admired his guile. She hunched her figure so that Thomas could see the sense in what Matthew said. He climbed up behind her and held her firmly. Whether Thomas thought Matthew was just giving him an excuse to also ride the mule, it did not matter so long as he accepted the ride in good grace. He slipped his arms around her waist and Matthew wrapped the blanket around both of them. Thomas rested his head on Phoebe's back and his eyes started to close.

'Will it be safe now?' Phoebe asked.

'Yes, the activity has long ceased,' Matthew answered as he led the donkey along a narrow path.

Phoebe looked into his eyes. Matthew was very well informed for a preacher riding a donkey in the night to be near to God. How? Daylight was only just breaking, so how did he know so soon? The path twisted and turned but the sure-footed mule did not falter.

'Why would a preacher be leading a

wagon in and out of a mill?' Phoebe asked. She fought the tired feeling that threatened to engulf her. Matthew was a puzzle to her. Kind? Yes, but honest — she had her doubts, despite Matthew's current attire. He was a man of more than one role, although he obviously meant them no harm.

'Helping a friend out who was unable to do his job,' Matthew answered, but kept his eyes firmly on the path as it peaked.

Phoebe and Thomas looked out in awe as the day, now dawning above a vast expanse of sea, revealed a large sweeping bay. Below them, down through even more trees that followed the brook's path as it ran down the valley, lay a small hamlet at the base of a headland. From their vantage point, they could see that, further along the bay, was a larger fishing village.

A small fleet of cobles, the local flat-bottomed fishing boats, nestled in its natural harbour. This coast was one of dramatic headlands, steep paths, and gently sweeping bays of flat sands. The sea was a wild changing beast, often treacherous with wild breakers and high tides, yet always beautiful.

'Is that Ebton?' Thomas asked, pointing to the larger village beyond the dunes that lined the lower coastal path.

'Yes. This, down here, is Scarbeck. My cottage nestles at the end of the gill, behind Gannet Nab — that's the round hill, just behind the Rowan Inn. It's sparse, but has a small stove that keeps it warm.' Matthew moved them on and, once more, darkness fell as they entered the cover of the trees.

As they neared the end of the path, a rider entered the woods. His uniform glistened in the daylight as it filtered through the thinner cover.

'Morning, preacher.' He nodded at Matthew and stared at the two figures on the mule. 'What are you doing out so early in the morning with those two?'

The soldier, a dragoon, Phoebe thought, stopped his horse in front of

Matthew and towered over them on the donkey. 'Looking after two homeless waifs, Sir. The war has been long and hard. It has taken many a father away from their poor homes. I'm taking those two in until I find them some work and a good Christian family.'

'You'll be havin' your work cut out for you then, Reverend, as there are plenty of folk around here who can't feed their own children, let alone the waifs of the dead. What be their names?' He looked suspiciously at Phoebe, 'Although you could catch yourself a man easy enough.'

'This chap is Didymus and his sister here is Florence.'

Phoebe glanced around at Matthew. He had bent the truth with Thomas's name but lied about hers. Was it a coincidence, or had he known that their mother's name was Florence? Thomas squeezed Phoebe's hand as he felt her take in a sharp breath on hearing her mother's name. She was also very annoyed at the sergeant's suggestion.

'Well, Didymus and Florence, keep your heads down and work hard. If you see anything strange happening around these parts, you come and tell me, Sergeant Hughes, at the garrison. I'll have some nice warm meat for you if you help us catch the local villains — smugglers, evil men. Now be on yer way. Good day to you, preacher.'

Matthew nodded and touched his hat. 'May God be with you, Sergeant.'

Matthew did not look back but walked them out on to a flat, sandy, open path. They stopped and he removed his hat and wiped the sweat from his brow on the back of his hand. He looked as though he was taking deep breaths of the fresh salty air. Phoebe climbed down and ran on to the fine soft sand. She laughed and spun around and Matthew grinned at her. She played like a child, not like the woman she was, the mill forgotten, her tiredness disappearing in her excitement.

'You lied, preacher man,' Thomas

said as he stood next to Matthew.

'The Lord forgive me. Yes, I did.' He looked down at Thomas who, for the first time, realised how tired Matthew was. He looked as if he had not slept all night either. 'Do you know why I lied, Thomas?'

Thomas shrugged his shoulders then grinned. 'To protect us.'

'Yes, boy, to protect the pair of you from your own foolishness. You will now be Didymus, and Phoebe will answer to Florence or Florrie. Don't slip or you might be taken back to the mill.'

Thomas agreed, then asked, 'Did you know my mother's name was Florence?'

Matthew turned the mule to follow the coastal path. 'No.' He looked surprised. 'Was it?' He kept going. 'Call your sister. We must get you to the safety of the cottage.'

Thomas turned and shouted, 'Ph . . . Florrie, we must go now.'

Phoebe hesitated for a moment but, at Thomas's familiar voice, she came. 'I think in time, I'll get used to that name, Didy.'

They smiled at each other and followed Matthew, listening to the roar of an angry sea, crashing distant waves and gulls cawing overhead. Phoebe thought she would like life here. It was as invigorating as the mill had been stifling.

They neared the high round hill and Matthew removed a slate from the ditch at the side of the path. He stooped down and picked up a bundle that was tucked behind a large rock. He said nothing to them but walked them around the small hill — the nab, to the cottage door. 'Go in. I'll see to Trojan.'

'Trojan?' Thomas said.

'Yes, he's as stubborn and unyielding as if he were made from hardwood,' Matthew said and grinned.

'The Trojan horse was also not what it appeared to be.' Phoebe's words seemed to take Matthew by surprise. His usual calm response was not there. Instead, he laughed and took the donkey behind the cottage.

Thomas lifted an eyebrow to his sister. 'So what is he?' he asked.

'A Trojan horse for sure, but a kind one that we can trust, Didy.' Phoebe's confidence was reassuring Thomas but, she sincerely hoped, was not misplaced.

They entered the small cottage, which was dark until Phoebe opened the shutters. It was sparse but they both looked longingly at the sight of a narrow bed, thinking of sleep.

'Florrie, how is your arm?' Matthew entered, shutting the door behind him. He poured them all a drink of milk from a churn inside the door.

'It aches but I think no more than it should do.' Phoebe looked at the sparse altar by the fire. 'We . . . I stole your honey.'

'No, you didn't. It was a gift, left to be taken.' Thomas watched the broad smile appear on Matthew's face when he saw Phoebe's relief.

'You will have to sleep on the cot

tonight. I shall sleep in the chair until I go out.'

'Go where?' Phoebe asked.

'Where I must,' Matthew replied, and then said no more.

7

Phoebe and Thomas slept most of the next day. When Thomas awoke in the middle of the night he found Phoebe peering out of the shutter in the window of the cottage. Heavy waves could be heard breaking on the shore.

'What are you watching, Phoebe?' he said as he rubbed his eyes trying to clear away the sleepy darkness.

'Quiet, Didy.' She was sitting on the stone windowsill. 'There is someone out there — and you're supposed to call me Florrie now.' Phoebe didn't turn her attention away from the gap.

'Sorry. Where's Matthew?' Thomas stepped out of the bed and walked over to the window. 'Ow!' He let out a curse as he stubbed his toe on the old table that was in the middle of the cottage floor.

'Shh!' Phoebe glanced around. 'I

think there is a boat cutting through the breakers. Look, over there.' Phoebe pointed out and Thomas screwed up his face as he also peered out into the night.

The moonlight glistened off the incoming waves. 'Surely the smugglers would not be out two nights running. The preventative officers would be watching for them.'

Thomas was watching a man jumping out of a small flat-bottomed boat, struggling against the waves as he pulled it up on to the beach. 'It's Matthew!'

'No, I don't believe it,' Phoebe retorted. 'Matthew is a good man.' Phoebe did not particularly want to argue with Thomas but she could not accept that Matthew was corrupted in any way, yet she did not understand what she had seen, either.

They watched in amazement as Matthew's figure emerged across the beach. Tall and straight as always, he was wearing a buttoned half jacket, loose trousers and the heavy oilskin boots of a fisherman. A dark wool hat was pulled firmly on to his head as he walked into the cold night wind across the flat sand. Another shorter man, dressed in a long black riding coat, greeted him. The two exchanged a few words and then Matthew was handed something before the man disappeared into the shadows again.

'He's coming! Quick, back to bed, Didy,' Phoebe said excitedly.

Both ran back to the cot, huddling under the blankets. A small fire still burned in the hearth, giving off a little heat and light. The door opened and they felt the rush of cold air enter the cottage. Matthew closed it, firmly bolting it behind him. Thomas peered out just enough to watch what Matthew was doing. He could smell the salt sea air on him. Then Matthew walked over to the window and firmly slammed the shutters together, fastening them securely.

Thomas and Phoebe sat up abruptly.

'What did you do that for?' Thomas asked, rubbing his eyes again as if he had just woken up.

'Because you didn't close it!' Matthew snapped.

'I didn't touch them!' Thomas said defiantly.

Matthew turned around so quickly that they both sat on the bed, leaning against the stone wall of the cottage.

'Listen, Didymus, I have helped you. I have fed you. Do not lie to me! You watched from the window. I saw the flickering firelight behind the shutter and so could anyone else out there this night. Here everyone keeps their shutters and door closed of a night. What you don't see can't hurt you. Remember that and you might live to be an adult!'

Matthew was pointing at him with the poker from the fire. He looked angry, but Phoebe did not feel frightened by him. 'He didn't lie, it was me who watched you,' Phoebe confessed.

'It is not for you to know or

understand anything.'

'You've lied before!' Thomas replied.

Matthew dropped the poker by the fire's hearth. 'Yes, God forgive me, I have, to save your impudent skin. No wonder Bladderwell was ready to tan your hide. You don't know how to control that mouth of yours.'

'It was me.' Phoebe's voice took Matthew by surprise. His anger seemed to disperse as soon as she spoke again.

'What was you?' Matthew asked.

'I was at the shutter. I saw you. It was me.' Phoebe looked at Matthew. 'I'm sorry. I wanted to watch the sea. I've never seen anything so wonderful. I wasn't spying on you.' She looked down at her hands.

'Oh, I see.' Matthew sat down in the chair and gently rocked it, as if he was thinking about what to do next. 'So what did you see, Phoebe?'

'You, your fishing boat. When I realised it was you stepping out I ran back to bed. I didn't want you to think I was watching you.' She looked at the fire, reflecting on just how much she did like watching him.

'Although you were. I'm sorry I snapped at you, Didy. I am tired and I'm not used to having dependents. I shall find you more suitable places to work and stay tomorrow,' Matthew told them.

'But why?' Phoebe stood up. 'We can stay and help you here. I could cook, clean and look after the donkey and Thomas could help you fish.'

Thomas was as surprised as Matthew at Phoebe's outburst. He had never been in a boat in his life and didn't particularly want to start now, particularly after seeing how much it moved.

'Phoebe, it simply is not suitable for you to stay here,' Matthew said dismissively.

'Why?' She walked over to him, standing by the firelight. Dressed in her breeches that were held up by a piece of rope, she looked like a street pedlar. At least she wore boots now and they actually fit her.

'Because you are a young woman who needs a woman to teach you what to do in this world. I am a single man who can no longer just strip off in front of a warm fire, wrap himself in his blankets, whilst his clothes dry. Besides, I don't need Thomas to help me fish because I'm not a fisherman.' Matthew put a comforting hand on her shoulder.

She stared at his face and sensation flowed through her that was both exciting and surely improper, yet she didn't care. She liked this man and wanted to help him in his secret world, whatever it was, as much as he apparently wanted to help them. As if reading her thoughts, he quickly withdrew his hands.

'What are you then?' Thomas asked defiantly.

'A preacher!' Matthew snapped back.

'You have forgotten I am not fit to work in a hall yet. My arm,' Phoebe offered the excuse.

Thomas looked suspiciously at her. It seemed as if she was trying anything she could to get out of leaving Matthew. Thomas's eyes betrayed a jealousy that she could sense yet chose to ignore. She was a woman and had no-one else in the world to consider but Thomas.

'Your arm is no more than scratched and sore. It was a surface cut that is healing cleanly, I am pleased to say.'

'Thanks to you,' Phoebe said softly.

'Perhaps so.' Matthew shifted uneasily on his chair and looked into the fire as if trying to escape the conversation.

'Here.' Phoebe pulled Thomas out of bed. She put two blankets on the table, the third she wrapped around herself and curled up on the bed facing the stone wall. 'I shall not look. You can still have your privacy.'

Matthew changed and for some time did not speak. 'I'm sorry, it is too dangerous for you two to stay here.'

'You are going to split us up, aren't you?' Phoebe said accusingly.

'I don't want to but, unless there is work for you both at the baker's cottage then your best chance will be at Sunnington Hall. Thomas will find work in the town, I'm sure.'

'Sunnington Hall. That's where Marwood works. I don't want to be anywhere near the man. He's a monster. He said he would sell me at the market. He said I'd fetch a good price!' Phoebe protested.

'Did he, the blackguard. He's a gamekeeper and a very efficient one,' Matthew said, but with an edge to his voice that betrayed his distaste of the man. 'Phoebe, no-one will sell or ill-treat you because I shall be around to check on your progress.'

Phoebe felt a rush of comfort flow through her body as she heard his words. He was not abandoning her. If only he looked upon her as she did him. Phoebe flushed at her thoughts.

'Tell me, Phoebe, how did your mother die?'

Phoebe was surprised by Matthew's question. It was such an abrupt change of subject and a very sensitive one. 'We don't really know. She took ill and was taken into the poorhouse. We were only supposed to work at the mill to pay for her keep until she was better, then we were all going to be together again. Only they came and said she'd died.' Phoebe heard Thomas swallow and he reached out for her hand.

'Was there a funeral?' Matthew asked in a gentle voice.

'No. Nothing.'

'Tell me where she was taken and I'll try and find out exactly what happened.' Matthew had dressed in his preacher's attire and wrapped himself in the blanket, sitting in the chair by the fire.

'Gumbel Beck Workhouse. I read it on the gate as they took her in.' Phoebe's voice was shaking slightly.

'It'll take a day for me to get there and back, but I promise I will make this journey for you so that you can have peace in your hearts before starting your new lives.'

Thomas and Phoebe went back to

bed. Phoebe lay there thinking of her mother, then wondering again about Matthew. What was the parcel he had picked up when they arrived at the cottage? Why would he go all the way to Gumbel Beck to find out about their mother? Nothing made sense to her.

In the morning, Phoebe showed Thomas the piece of paper she found in the hearth of the cottage.

Phoebe stood up. 'No matter what Matthew is, one thing is for sure, we have two mysteries to solve. What Matthew really is, and if Levi lives, or did the batman with the blackthorn club, kill him?'

8

'Look!' Thomas held up a slate, which had been left on the table. Phoebe read the words written on it. *Stay here. Do not leave the cottage. Help yourself to the food. Await my return. M.*

Phoebe studied the writing carefully then placed it back on the table thoughtfully. 'He is an educated man, his writing is even and well-formed.'

'Priests are supposed to be, aren't they?' Thomas said sarcastically.

'Why don't you like Matthew?'

'Why do you like him so much?' Thomas snapped back at her.

'I trust him.'

'Yes, you'd rather follow Matthew's advice than mine.'

Phoebe knew he wanted to be the man in the family now. He needed her to look to him for strength.

'We'll have our food and then we'll

go on our way,' Thomas announced defiantly as he cut into a loaf of bread.

'Didy! Did you not hear what I read out? We are to stay here.' Phoebe glared at him angrily and she saw he hated that also.

'Why? Just because he said so? I don't think that's a good enough reason. He could be a French spy for all we know. He snoops around in the dark and receives packages on the beach. Think about it, Phoebe, what else could he be?'

'He is our friend, Didy. He has helped us and, besides . . . ' she stopped mid sentence and handed Thomas his food, ' . . . we need him. We have no homes, no jobs,' Phoebe sighed, 'and no family. What's more we're wanted for wrecking, so what chance do we have of surviving on our own?'

'You might need him. I don't.' Thomas walked over to the door. 'I'm going. Are you coming with me or staying here with Matthew, Phoebe?' He was being unreasonable. Deep down he knew it, but pride would not let him back down.

'Didy, I'm not going unless I know where it is you intend to take us and why?' Phoebe crossed her arms. He stormed out of the cottage door slamming it shut behind him.

Outside on his own Thomas felt emptiness in the pit of his stomach. He was alone, staring across the flat sand to the breaking waves with white horses lifting high then crashing down against each other.

'I tell you, he is your man, Lieutenant.' A loud irate voice bellowed across the open beach to Thomas's ears.

Thomas ran back to the cottage before anyone saw him.

'Didy, you've come to your senses. I knew you would. What . . . ' Phoebe crouched next to him by the window as he frantically put his finger to his lips to tell her to be quiet.

'Who is it?'

'I don't know.' Thomas ran to the fire to grab the poker when he accidentally tripped, falling on to the hearth. He looked up feeling the warmth of a dying fire in front of his face. 'Thank you, God!' he said as he had narrowly missed stumbling headfirst into the hot ashes. He sat up and looked at the floor where he had caught his toe. The cottage had a rough wooden floor. One plank was raised slightly above the others. He crawled over to it and lifted it to reveal a small hiding place — an empty hiding place. He placed the plank back carefully so it fitted true to the floor.

'Phoebe . . . '

'I swear I saw him last night, I tell you.' The voice was louder and coming nearer. The person spoke with authority.

'Dragoons, Phoebe,' Thomas whispered as the men pounded on the door.

'Didy, quickly hide here.' Phoebe who was holding a small oil lamp pushed hard against the wall to the right of the fire. 'Help me!' The dragoons were shouting for Matthew to open up and let them in. The solid-looking wall moved smoothly, and they soon found themselves inside a narrow passage. They quickly pushed the panel back securely and listened.

'How did you know about this?' Thomas whispered.

'I saw Matthew go out this way.' Phoebe held the small lamp up. It flickered against the walls of the roughly hewn passage.

'I can see.' Thomas had his face against a small spy hole, which he had found in the wall. 'It's a preacher — a proper one.'

'Can you hear anything, Didy?' Phoebe was leaning close to him. The small light flickered and the cold draught that came up from the passage chilled both of them.

Thomas put his ear to the hole and listened carefully.

'I tell you, Lieutenant, the man is your spy. He was seen last night with an accomplice.' The accusing voice was from the short rotund figure of the

Reverend Hickworth from the local church of St Cuthbert and of the Sunnington Estates.

'We'll search this cottage, but I tell you this is all highly irregular. Listen to me, Archibald, I know someone is selling secrets to the French, but we need proof, not wild accusations! Are you sure you are not just trying to remove him because he is a Methodist and preaching to your ever dwindling flock?'

'How dare you. If you were not my own flesh and blood, George, I would complain to your superior officer for such insolence!' The Reverend's face was red with anger.

'Of course, but if I was not your flesh and blood you could not come to me with such an outlandish tale and expect me to search a cottage without my superior's knowledge, could you? Besides, who was it that saw him and why were they out that late at night themselves?'

The Reverend stepped back as two

dragoons came in and searched the cottage. It did not take them long, sparse as it was. 'I am told things in confidence that I can not repeat.'

'How very convenient for you,' the Lieutenant said pointedly.

Thomas looked at Phoebe as one of the dragoons came towards the wall. He had been leaning gently on various panels as if testing them for secret hiding places. He pushed on the hidden trap door and they pressed with all their might against it. It held firm and the soldier walked away, completely unaware of how close he had been to discovering them.

They both sighed with relief as the men left the cottage. 'What do we do now, Didy?' Phoebe asked.

'We had better tell Matthew about this and ask him who and what he really is. Would you shelter a French spy?' Thomas asked, obviously pleased that at last he would make his sister see reason.

'How do we explain that we weren't

discovered by them? Remember it is he who is harbouring two runaway machine breakers. So who should tell who about whom?' Phoebe's reply visibly shocked Thomas with its truth. They were all outlaws.

'We'll find out where this leads. That way we can still return to the cottage before he does.' Thomas took the small lamp and stepped forward. He had not taken more than ten steps when the ground, which was sandy and uneven became rocky and slippery. Phoebe had to stoop uneasily so as not to bang her head. Only the sound of dripping water and their breath broke the silence.

The passage lowered and turned sharply. It split into two separate tunnels. They followed the lower one and nearly fell into the sea beneath them as the path gave way to a steep set of steps leading down to a hidden cave in the headland. A small fishing boat was moored beneath where they were standing.

'Well, we know one place where our

fishing preacher comes and goes from,' Phoebe said, then looked back the way they had come.

'Let's try the high passage and see where it takes us,' Thomas agreed excitedly.

They walked carefully back to where the passage started to climb up. Phoebe guessed they were following the line of the gill but they changed directions so many times that she was losing her bearings. Eventually they finally came to a trap door, but both were quite breathless.

'What do we do now?' Thomas asked.

'Open it?' Phoebe said but wasn't sure. 'Slowly.'

Slowly Thomas lifted the trap door. A piece of sackcloth seemed to be laid over it. He pushed it a little higher and could see a cobbled floor in front of him and what seemed to be the inside of a stable block. He could smell horses and heard a whinny. Memories of their old farm horse, Merlin, came rushing back to him.

He heard voices and quickly lowered the door until he could only just see the hooves and boots of the horses held by the two men.

'When will Levi have the stuff ready?' a gruff voice asked.

'Soon, he's promised it soon. He's gone to meet the governor today. Said he'll be back before nightfall. If he sets this one up it will be the biggest yet.' The voice sounded familiar.

'Well I have to get back meself. I told his Lordship I have to go to Ebton this afternoon to pick her Ladyship's new shoes — as if she needs any more!'

'Our preacher should do a sermon for the likes of the idle rich, on greed, eh?' said the faceless voice.

The other man muttered in agreement as he mounted one of the horses and rode out into the yard.

Thomas wondered which preacher he was talking about — Matthew or the Reverend Hickworth. Who was Levi?

'What is it, Didy? I have to get out of

here.' Phoebe was tugging at Thomas's waistcoat.

Thomas lifted the door carefully and slid out. There was no-one around so he helped Phoebe out. They crawled into the far corner of the stable nearest the yard.

'Look, Didy.' Phoebe pointed across the yard from the stable.

'Sunnington Hall!' Thomas exclaimed as they stared across the perfectly-laid garden and lake at the back of the magnificent grand Hall.

9

Thomas and Phoebe peered around the large stable door, across to the back of the Palladian house. It was so grand and symmetrical — everything about it at one side seemed to extend and match the building at the other.

The whole building was the focal point of a vast expanse of cleared ground — laid to lawn, lake and follies designed by someone like Lancelot Capability Brown.

'Does the Prince Regent himself visit here, Phoebe?' Thomas's voice seemed tiny and insignificant just as she herself felt against grandeur on such a vast scale.

'Oh Didy, to be able to live like this!' Phoebe said in amazement. 'It would be immoral.'

'Anyone with a conscience would not sleep at night until everyone in the land at least had a dry warm bed and food in their belly!' Thomas snapped the words out in a moment of rage.

'Let's go now before we're caught.' Thomas turned to go back to the trap door when he saw a figure he knew so well, and hated — Seth Barton. He was heading for the old church behind what looked like the herb garden, near the kitchens. They quickly ran behind and around the bushes that grew by the stone parameter wall. They saw him head into the church via the main wooded archway. Bending low and keeping to the shadows where possible, they entered the church gates.

'What's he doing here?' Thomas asked quietly, not expecting an answer, but, like Phoebe, determined to find out.

'More to the point, what are you doing here?' The voice came from a girl dressed like a scullery maid.

Thomas and Phoebe spun around. Both were ready to make a break for it when two words came from Thomas's mouth. 'Help us!'

The girl's emerald eyes widened and an unruly auburn curl escaped her white cap.

Seth Barton appeared in the doorway of the church, Phoebe and Thomas crouched low behind the wooden gate, out of his vision but dependent on the will of the shocked scullery maid. 'What d'yer want, girl? Who was yer speakin' to?' Seth's tone was harsh as always.

'I was lookin' for the Reverend Hickworth, Sir. Cook says there is some cake waitin' for him when he has a moment.' As soon as Seth disappeared inside the church again, she bent as if to fasten her boot and said pointedly to Thomas, 'Tell me what you're doin' here or I'll scream so loud I'll have Levi himself down on yer.'

Thomas replied instantly. 'Who is Levi?'

'What d'yer want to know for?' Her eyes bore down on Thomas.

'I don't know anything about him

other than we want to find him. Who's Levi? I must find him.' Thomas saw the girl's face pale.

'You is odd, boy. Go away and don't come back. Take yer sister with you, and don't ask again about Levi. What yer don't know can't do yer any harm.' She was shaking. What Thomas had said had definitely upset her, yet she put on as calm a face as she could.

'Who are you?' Thomas asked quickly as the girl stood straight brushing down her skirts.

'Mercy! Mercy Bright! Where are you, you lazy girl?' Cook appeared at the scullery doorway and the girl shouted back to her at once.

'Go! Go away and don't come back unless yer goin' to tell us who you are and what you're about.' The girl ran straight for the house.

Thomas scratched his head. Then he grinned slightly. 'Let's find out. I bet Seth Barton is in the thick of whatever is going on here, don't you?'

Phoebe nodded and followed Thomas

as they slipped behind a large gravestone. 'We can make our way slowly around to the side door.'

In silence they scurried like a pair of squirrels across the ground until they were at the side of the church.

'Phoebe, she had a very strong accent,' Thomas said. 'Don't you think it's odd that her accent is so heavy?'

'No, not if she's pretending. People who try to copy an accent often overdo it. Perhaps she shouldn't really be here either. She didn't look very much like a scullery maid to me.'

Once inside the church they stayed on their hands and knees filtering between the upright wooden pews.

Thomas pointed to the side chapel where Seth Barton was sitting. He did not strike them as a religious man, more of one who was bored whilst waiting for someone to arrive.

They were halfway across the aisle when they heard the large oak door at the front of the church open. Quickly, without waiting to see who was entering, they rolled under the altar cloth. Whoever it was walked purposefully up the aisle and knelt down in front of the altar.

'What brings you here?' The voice sounded angry as if the man was barely in control of his temper. Thomas recognised it instantly as the voice of the Reverend Hickworth.

'I thought you were goin' to get rid of the preacher man, Matthew? He arrived at the mill this mornin'. I tell yer he's always snoopin' around there. With respect, Rev, what priest will muck in and help do a sick man's work like he does?'

A good one, thought Phoebe.

Hickworth grunted. 'Aye, I was going to have him removed, but he'd already gone. He's taken the package with him, too!' The Reverend shifted his weight uneasily. 'I'll put paid to him soon enough. If he is too clever for Levi to catch out, then I'll have to find his Achilles' heel.' The Reverend spoke with malice and loathing in his words.

Hardly what you'd expect from a man of the church, Phoebe thought.

'Let me deal with him,' Barton offered.

'No! His family is far too influential for that. We'd have every dragoon between York and Newcastle upon us. Business would stop completely. No, the way to deal with the likes of him is to bring shame on him and his family. His father may not want to see Matthew for what he has done, but deep down he has respect for the man and his principles.

'Now you go and don't you ever come back here again unless I send for you — do you understand me, Barton?' The Reverend's voice was cold.

'Aye, clear enough.'

Seth was half way down the aisle when the Reverend Hickworth shouted to him, 'What of those rascals who broke the machines — any news of them?'

'Don't know what happened to them, but I do know the machines were replaced real quick and the search called off. Those brats were bought fair and square from the master and mistress of the workhouse, yet they let them off. If Ben gets his hands on them again they'll end up as fish fodder. Good day, Reverend.' Barton left.

Thomas and Phoebe were holding hands tightly waiting expectantly for Hickworth to go, but he stayed for a further ten minutes. Phoebe's mind was reeling. How did we come to be bought? We were there because Mother died. It didn't make sense, something was very wrong and who would pay to replace the machines? No-one they knew had any money or influence.

'Ah, Jethro, I'm glad you are safe,' Reverend Hickworth greeted an uncouth looking man who had entered the church. 'I have a little job for you. Seth took it upon himself to visit me here, in the sanctity of this house of God. It was a fatal misjudgement on his part — one that we cannot tolerate! I think he should have taken a lot more

110

care, particularly when working with those machines. See to it that he learns his lesson well — once and for all.' The Reverend left and the man, Jethro, nodded and followed him.

Thomas and Phoebe ran through the graveyard back to the stable block only to find it swarming with grooms and horses. They had no choice but to climb up a tree, then over the high wall and back on to the coast road that would take them back through the gill.

'What do we do?' Phoebe asked, and then continued to answer her own question. 'We must tell him all. He is in great danger. Perhaps he knows who Levi is?'

Thomas stopped to catch his breath when they reached the cover of the trees. 'We are free, Phoebe. We don't have to hide anymore. Unless we see Bladderwell of course.'

'But what about Matthew? He helped us, Didy.' Phoebe looked at her brother. 'What about Mercy? If she's pretending to be what she's not, she may need

Matthew's help even if we don't. And Didy, how did we come to be brought from the workhouse?'

'I don't know, Phoebe, but you're right. We'd best get back to the cottage quickly before Matthew, or else it could be too late.'

They ran nearly the whole way down to the sandy beach to the cottage. It took them almost all the afternoon. Phoebe realised just how much of a short-cut the tunnel was.

With great relief they opened the cottage door and nearly dropped with exhaustion to be faced by Matthew sitting in his chair, rocking and staring intently at them. Before either of them spoke, they saw the oil lamp in his hands. Phoebe watched as he placed it on the table. She was riddled with guilt. She'd left it by the entrance to the trap door in the stable. Anyone could have found it and then his secret tunnel would have been discovered.

She also realised they had nearly given the Reverend Hickworth the evidence he craved to have Matthew arrested. No wonder he looked at them with blind fury in his eyes.

'What have you got to say for yourselves?' Matthew was standing, with his hands placed firmly on the table in front of him. 'I told you to stay here and await my return. You can read, Phoebe. You must have found the slate.' When they had heard the voices, Phoebe had panicked and dropped it on the floor. Fortunately, the soldiers had not bothered picking it up.

'If we'd stayed we would've been discovered, and may even have been forced to speak out against you!' she answered defiantly. Her head was filled with all the things they had seen and heard. She wanted to tell Matthew everything and at last find out who and what he was.

'By whom?' Matthew was obviously surprised by her answer.

Phoebe noted too, that instead of asking why they should have to speak against him, Matthew's response was to ask by whom. 'By the Reverend Hickworth and his relative in the dragoons. They came to find what it was you were given on the beach last night. He said you were spying for the French.' Phoebe watched Matthew's expression change. A cynical smile appeared on his face then he rubbed his head and placed his hands on his waist, flicking his black jacket behind him.

'So how did you know about the tunnel?' he asked.

'I watched you go through it,' Phoebe interrupted. 'If I hadn't, Matthew, we would've been found.'

He nodded in agreement. 'So you think I'm a spy, Thomas?' he asked without looking at the boy.

'No, you're not,' Phoebe answered positively. She could no more believe that this man who had helped and cradled her in his arms was capable of such a lowly act.

'What about you, Thomas?' Matthew asked.

Thomas replied swiftly, 'I'm sure

you're not a spy. But you're not what you appear to be.'

Something in the back of Phoebe's mind was telling her she had missed something obvious about him.

Matthew sat down in the chair. 'Thank you for that, at least. No, I'm not a French spy, but these are dangerous parts and desperate men surround us. Now tell me what adventure you had beyond the tunnel.'

Phoebe and Thomas both told Matthew all about their extraordinary day. He listened intently. They did not mention the scullery maid. They did not think she would tell anyone she had seen them, anyway.

'So — did anyone see you?' Matthew asked again.

Phoebe smiled. 'Yes, Mercy Bright, but you already knew that or who would've brought you the lamp back down. She knows about this place, doesn't she? You're working together, aren't you?'

Phoebe was pleased that she had

figured out part of the puzzle, but an uneasy feeling swept through her — who or what was Mercy Bright to Matthew?

'You already know far more than it is safe. I am going to take you to a place of safety — a house where you will be fed, clothed respectably, and where no-one will question your presence. You will stay there until I finish my business here. Then we shall talk openly.' Matthew picked up a leather bag and swung it over his shoulder.

Phoebe had been thumbing frantically through a bible but, before she found what she was looking for, Matthew had lit a lamp and opened the secret door.

'Do you have to go now?' Phoebe asked wearily. 'We have hardly eaten all day and we've walked miles to get back here. Can't it wait until morning?'

'No, unfortunately, but you can sleep in the boat,' Matthew said as he closed the panel behind them.

'Boat!' Thomas exclaimed. 'No, I

don't think we should, it could be dangerous! You could get shot at.'

'Thomas we have little choice in the matter. Now follow in silence, please.' Matthew led them down the passage, taking the turning that led to the steep stairs to the cove. The boat was still tethered at the bottom. They both stepped warily inside. Thomas moved to the far end where a piece of oilcloth covered some boxes.

Matthew untied the boat and steered it with the oars. 'There are some food supplies in the top box — help yourself to something. We have to go down the coast to a small hamlet. It is not far but the sea is a treacherous mistress and I'll take you there as swiftly and calmly as I can.'

'Seth Barton said we were bought, Matthew. How can that be?' Phoebe asked.

'It is a sad fact that workhouses do sell on children, and sometimes women for all manner of work, be it factory or chimney sweep. A child without an adult's caring protection is, in this day and age, a sad, vulnerable commodity.'

'It is no better than slavery. It should be abolished also.' Thomas spoke with feeling. 'When I grow up, somehow I will try to help those less fortunate than myself.'

Phoebe smiled at him proudly, but the only trouble was, unless his circumstances took a huge turn for the better, there weren't many more desolate than they were, if it were not for their mysterious friend.

'So what of our mother; could she possibly be alive still?' Phoebe shouted above the roar of the waves. Hope filled her heart.

'No Florence Elgie was listed in the poorhouse books. They denied she was ever there.' Matthew pulled hard to manoeuvre the boat to follow the line of the coast. His eyes seemed to watch everywhere for signs of activity.

'So where is she?' Phoebe asked. 'She's alive — I know it! Perhaps she was listed under her maiden name?'

'I sincerely hope so, Phoebe, but I checked the entries and couldn't find a Florence Fenton either. It will take a little time to find out where she is.'

'How did you know her surname?' Thomas asked. 'We've never said.'

Matthew smiled at him. 'You are very quick, young Thomas. I knew her once, a long time ago. And you my beautiful Phoebe, you look the image of her.' Matthew was heading for a small hamlet built on to the side of the steep cliffs. Few lamps lit it from open windows, but with the light of the moon they could see the tiny harbour.

Phoebe watched him hardly daring to believe he had called her, 'my beautiful Phoebe'. Had he realised what he had said?

Matthew pulled the boat on to a small slipway and fastened it to an iron ring fixed into the wall. He signalled for them to move slowly and silently. Instead of making for the main street, he took them through the narrowest of gaps between two houses, then down a few steps and under a slab and into a tunnel.

After quite a time, Matthew started to climb a ladder. He continued until he had released the door at the top. Then, as light flickered down upon them, he came back down to help Phoebe and Thomas.

They emerged from the tunnel into a grand conservatory, which had plants growing on each column between the huge panes of glass. Lamps lit the whole room — the conservatory was a fashionable place where people could walk indoors whilst having the feeling of being outdoors. Only a large house would have such an extravagance added to it. Matthew fastened the door securely and then covered it with the rush matting again.

'Where are we?' Thomas asked as his mouth gaped open.

'This is Hawksey Manor,' Matthew said.

'And this is private property. Unless you have the permission of the owner

— namely myself — to be here, then I believe you are trespassing, my boy.' The voice came from a tall well-dressed gentleman holding a pistol in his hand.

Thomas ran to Matthew's side. He was looking for the nearest door to escape through. They were all too far away. The one they had just entered by was firmly shut. They were trapped!

'Welcome would have been a more commodious greeting, Father,' Matthew said dryly.

'Father!' Thomas repeated.

'The prodigal returns. Are you to offer to be my slave to make up for your departure and the loss of my heir, or am I to greet you with open arms and celebrate,' the man said sarcastically, yet Phoebe could sense an unspoken bond and respect existed between these two men.

'Do these . . . belong to you?' the man asked.

'Not exactly, no. They are the culprits from the mill. I sent you word of them, Father,' Matthew added.

'Yes, I got your word and it was done. Costly your 'words', preacher man! So what do you want of me now?'

'They need your help,' Matthew said flatly and stared directly at the older man's face.

'Who needs my help? You'll have to excuse me, my son, my ears aren't what they were.' The man smiled broadly at his son.

Matthew shifted uncomfortably. 'I need your help to hide and protect these young people. They've had enough trauma in their lives to deal with.' He looked at Phoebe. Their eyes met in an understanding of caring and mutual trust.

'Matthew, my boy.' He held out both arms open wide. 'Why didn't you tell me you were in trouble and needed me to help you? Of course I will, you only had to say!'

Matthew came forward and hugged his father closely. Thomas and Phoebe could see the older man's eyes almost fill with tears.

'Come! Come!' They were led back inside the house to the salon, which was a large open room designed to accommodate parties of people. 'After you.' Matthew's father tapped the frame of a huge painting. It released a door that led to carpeted staircase. They all walked up the stairs and he closed the doorway behind them. They seemed to come to a dead end.

Matthew leant over them and pulled on a small lever. A panel lifted before them. Thomas was the first to step into a cosy room with a huge fire burning in an ornate fireplace. A selection of chairs, draped in fine tapestry throws, were placed around it. All the other walls were covered in bookcases.

Matthew closed the panel behind them and pulled a cord to summon a servant. His father sat them together in one large chair next to the fire and pointed, insistently, to the other one for Matthew, who was reluctant to sit down, but his father pointed again, firmly, and he dutifully obeyed.

A servant promptly arrived. 'Fetch some warm milk and brandy, a selection of cold meats, soup and some cake.' His father dismissed the servant and then stood with his back to the fire.

'How did you know we were coming, Sir?' Thomas asked.

'Matthew pulled a chain in the tunnel that rings a warning bell in the house. After all, I don't want any uninvited guests now, do I?' He glanced furtively at his son.

'Have you seen the sense of this ridiculous feud, Father?' Matthew asked with a gruff voice.

'My son, I saw the sense of it not long after you left, but you move around so much in your different guises, I had to wait for you to need me again.'

'I've always needed you and your blessing upon me.' Matthew looked at Phoebe and Thomas who sat listening to this extremely personal conversation. Thomas shifted uneasily.

'Forgive me, I forget my manners. This is Phoebe and Thomas, and this is Lord Fenton, owner of Hawksey Manor.'

10

'Are you our grandfather?' Phoebe asked in disbelief. The thought had run through her mind, but she hardly dare voice it. Fenton was their mother's maiden name. It appeared highly unlikely and even possibly an arrogant suggestion, but how far, she wondered, could coincidences stretch. Why else would he pay for the broken machines?

Lord Fenton put a gentle hand on each of their heads. 'God forgive me, but I am. Had it not been for Matthew and his work I should never have known of your existence. I'm so sorry. I shall make it up to you both. From now on, this will be your home. You shall love it as your mother before you did.' He smiled at them and rubbed their heads gently. He then wiped his hands discreetly on his breeches and pulled the cord for the servant to return.

Phoebe was consumed with embarrassment at the state the two of them were in. Then another feeling surged around her veins — one that made her feel quite sick. If Lord Fenton were her grandfather and Matthew's father, then she was Matthew's niece! She had feelings for her own uncle!

'Bartholomew, have some water brought to Florence's old room. Phoebe and Thomas need a bathtub, clean nightwear and a soft warm bed. Come back as soon as the room is ready for them and send young Millie to help them when the tub is ready.'

'Why did you send us away that first night along the north road, if you knew who we were?' Thomas directed the question to Matthew, sternly.

'I didn't know your surname then. Remember, I was trying to get you away from harm. The cottage was to be used for an important meeting between two powerful men, and the contraband had arrived earlier than anticipated, which meant you needed to be far away from the path of the tubmen and the batman,' Matthew explained as if it should all be instantly apparent to them what was happening around them that night.

'But what are you?' Thomas persisted. 'You're no priest!'

'No, boy, that is where you are wrong. Matthew is a priest. As the younger son of mine, he was trained as a priest in the Church of England, a highly-respected position and one befitting his rank. It was a decision I made for him, as every father would like to guide his son wisely.' Lord Fenton sighed and gazed at the fire.

'His elder brother, William, had the calling for God, but I pressed him into the forces. I purchased him a commission. How was I to know we were about to enter a major war with Napoleon Bonaparte?' He glanced at Matthew. 'I did what I did to protect the family name. In the process, one by one, I lost my family.'

'Is William still fighting out there?'

Thomas asked. 'Our father was, but they said he was presumed dead.'

'No, Thomas. His battles are all done. He was not military material. Too soft. No, he died, I am told, the death of a hero leading his men into glory.' The man laughed an empty laugh filled with self-mockery. 'I was lost, devastated, when I heard, as I am sure you must have been over the death of your father. Before William died your mother fell in love with a worker on the estate — well below her station in life. A good man, honourable and hard working. After having had to fight with both of my sons to have them fulfil their rightful stations in life, I was not prepared to listen to the ranting of a young innocent girl, deeply in love.

'I'd adopted her from birth as my own when I married her dear mother. Matthew and William's mother died after a terrible riding accident. Phoebe, you are the image of your mother. I had found her a suitor — a man of means, someone I thought would care for her as well as I thought I had. Oh, he represented the new money of trade, but I was comfortable about that because I admired the man's foresight and abilities.

'He had introduced technology to the cotton industry and within five years had built ten mills throughout the north of England. He seemed a perfect catch — young, dashing, ambitious for a title and keen to marry into an old family. But Flo loved William Elgie and would not have him.'

'Did Mother elope with Father?' Phoebe asked. The idea was so appealing to her that they were truly in love. She tried not to look at Matthew but he turned to her and seemed to be staring at her.

'Yes. She knew what she wanted and she ruined her reputation and marred that of the family by doing it, but not without help.' He looked directly at Matthew.

'I had a friend marry them in secret. I helped her because I could not bear to have her spirit crushed by a man she loathed.' Matthew looked soberly at his father.

'Me?' She loathed me?' The older man's face looked shocked.

'No! She hated James Bartholomew Atkins. She saw him for what he was. A greedy, mean brute who cared nothing for the people who worked in his mills.' Matthew placed his hand on his father's shoulder.

Thomas and Phoebe followed the tale, fascinated as they munched the food hungrily from the tray. Thomas felt warmer and fuller than he had for weeks.

'The room is ready, my Lord.'

They looked longingly at the tray that still had a silver jug of milk and cakes left on it. 'Phoebe and Thomas, follow Millie. She will wash you, Thomas and put you to bed. I'll have the tray sent up in case you are still hungry in the night.'

'What about my mother? And why, if you're a priest, Matthew, do you masquerade as a Wesleyan — a Methodist?' Phoebe asked.

'I became a Methodist because I wanted to reach out and help those less fortunate than I have been in my life. If your mother, my sister, Florence, is alive, I shall find her. I give you my word on that, Phoebe and Didymus. Now enjoy your tub and sleep well.'

They followed the maid to the bottom of the stairs. She and Thomas seemed to strike up a conversation easily, so Phoebe stepped back quietly to the door and listened intently.

'Father, I am sorry I disobeyed you, but I'm not at all sorry that I helped Florence.' Matthew's voice was gentle but firm.

'I know your intentions were well meant, Matthew, but what has become of her? If Atkins is responsible for her ruin or death, I'll not stop with the law. I'll kill him with my own hands!' Lord Fenton's voice rose.

'I have to return tonight. I shall change and then finish the job I started before I stumbled upon them.' Matthew was telling his father what he intended to do.

'Matthew, I've lost a son and do not know the whereabouts of my beloved Flo. I don't want to lose you the same way. Stay here and let me send for the dragoons. You don't need to do this sort of thing anymore.'

'Father, if you send to the garrison, you will seal the fate of myself and two others. I do this work because it helps us win the war. There are traitors on our shores and I have to flush them out or they could bring down our country. I shall return father, I promise. Keep your faith in God and me.'

'Matthew, I may have doubted God over the years, forgive me that, but I've never doubted you — ever.'

Both men turned as Phoebe pushed the door open wide. 'You are Levi! I should have realised it. In the bible, Matthew and Levi were the same person — like you. I'd found you all along. Thomas is also called Didymus and Matthew, called Levi — I should have figured it out. You're a spy, but not for the French — you're one of ours.' Phoebe walked up to Matthew and held out her hand to him. 'I'm sorry if I ever doubted you.'

'Did you?'

'Never,' she replied honestly.

He smiled back at her, slightly embarrassed, but then kissed her hand and, for a moment, they looked at each other and Phoebe saw it was with a mutual longing.

A flustered maid appeared at the doorway, bobbing curtseys and making apologies for letting one of her charges eavesdrop.

'See to Thomas, Millie. I shall bring Phoebe to you in a moment.' Matthew smiled at her and the maid left, shutting the door behind her.

'Yes, Phoebe, that is correct. I have work to do and little time in which to do it.' Matthew released her hand. 'You must stay here and look after Thomas for me.'

'Your life is in danger. They want you to finish the deal and then I think the Reverend Hickworth will realise who you are.' Phoebe sighed. 'Who is Mercy Bright?' Phoebe asked and noticed the older man's eyebrows raise at the name of Mercy. She instantly felt threatened and jealous.

'Mercy is an old friend, and her sister, Sarah, was murdered by the gangs of smugglers who work around Stangcliffe.' At the mention of Mercy, his father had shifted uneasily. 'Father, she is a girl who comes from a good family. There is much I need to do. Get your rest and I'll see you before I go, I promise, all right?'

'You give me your word. You swear!' Phoebe tapped his preacher's collar.

'I do, now go.' Matthew watched her depart, and Phoebe felt proud of him, and a deep sense of longing within her.

It was early in the morning when Matthew, dressed not as a preacher, but as a man of the night, came to their bedroom. He had a black neckerchief

135

around his collar and pistols in his belt. A cutlass hung from a scabbard.

'I'm going now, Phoebe,' Matthew's voice whispered into her ear. She stirred and was instantly aware of his words.

'Will you not reconsider?'

'No, there are others relying on me, Phoebe.' He ran his fingers through her freshly-washed hair and smelled its freshness. He kissed her cheek and she instinctively turned her mouth to his. A fleeting kiss lingered and became a passionate embrace. Phoebe lost all thought of where she was or who he was to her. He was Matthew and she loved him despite all else and, as his lips pressed firmly and hungrily against hers, she knew he felt the same. He desired her too.

'Be safe, Levi.' Phoebe put her hand on his cheek but was surprised how swiftly he left.

Slowly, Phoebe's mind turned over all manner of thoughts in her head, the events of the last few weeks, then she sat bolt upright. She had to go with him. She had to follow. If Matthew was injured then she, too, had to be in the boat to help him.

'Thomas! Thomas! Wake up! I have to follow Matthew!'

Thomas woke and listened to his sister explain what was happening, then jumped down from the bed and searched around in the half-light for his clothes.

Phoebe quickly explained that she thought Matthew was heading for an ambush and needed her help. She stood up and found something with which to tie back her hair.

Phoebe thought quickly. 'Thomas, wait until I have gone then, when morning breaks, ask his Lordship to make sure that Mercy is brought safely here. If we suspect her as an impostor it will only be time before she, too, is in danger. Do this for Matthew and I'll warn him.'

Thomas looked at the uncertain expression on Phoebe's face. 'Trust me

Thomas, this is meant to be. I'll see Matthew safe and you find Mother. Matthew thinks he can do this all on his own. He can't. Once he has the evidence he seeks he will need outside help. Atkins might have a grudge against Mother. If he knew she rejected him for a pauper he may have her secreted away somewhere. Ask Lord Fenton to go to Gumbel Beck Workhouse or check out the local asylums. If money was paid for her to be put in one, his money could buy her out again.'

11

Phoebe ran, slipped and stumbled her way out into the street that Matthew had brought them to. It was dark and she had to stop for a moment to study all the narrow alleyways surrounding her. Phoebe's keen sense of direction led her back to the harbour. She inched her way around the wall of the noisy inn, heaving as it was with local fishermen.

The raucous laughs of the barmaids drifted out into the cobbled street. Phoebe peered along the line of boats, but she froze on the spot, as Matthew's wasn't there. Her heart quickened as she thought she had missed him. Then movements caught her eye, she looked to the sea.

Matthew was pushing the boat through the receding breakers. She nearly shouted out to him, but stopped herself remembering she was helping a spy and therefore had to use common sense and stealth.

Phoebe ran across the wet rocks covered in slippery moss and seaweed. She almost fell several times but somehow made it to the water's edge. Taking high leaping strides through the freezing cold water she neared him. Matthew jumped into the boat and turned to pick up the oars.

Suddenly he launched himself at the figure who was hanging on to the back of the boat trying to climb aboard. Phoebe thought for one awful moment that he was going to crack her skull with an oar, but Matthew realised just in time who she was. With one strong arm, he lifted her bodily into the boat, cursing at her the whole time.

'What in God's name do you think you are doing here?'

'Phoebe gasped and shivered on the boat's floor trying to regain her composure. 'Remember you are a man of the cloth, Matthew,' Phoebe said cheekily.

'I don't have the time to take you back. Didn't you listen to a word I said to you in the house? Don't you realise how dangerous my work is?'

Matthew was rowing frantically towards the headland. The sea was rougher than it had been when they came. Phoebe swallowed several times. She sat bolt upright, gripping tightly to the side of the boat as it dipped in the valley of each swell then raised on to the peak before being brought low again. 'I understand more than you do. That is why I came to rescue you.'

Matthew laughed and raised his voice so he could be heard above the rough sea. Waves crashed around them sending tall fingers of spray grasping frantically for the sky before falling back to the deep watery depths. Phoebe breathed in deeply, letting the salt air fill her lungs. This is what life should be like; a challenge — no walls, the right to taste freedom.

She watched Matthew, staring at the man who was rowing with all his strength for the shelter of the cove. 'This boat is heading for an ambush. They are on to you — they could be waiting by Stangcliffe, Matthew. If you head to the cove you'll be shot at for sure. Hickworth wants you dead!' Phoebe shouted the words with such conviction that Matthew paused, held the boat where they were and pulled out a spyglass.

'Damnation!' He turned the boat and rowed parallel to the shore. 'I don't know how you knew, Phoebe, but you and your instincts have my thanks.'

'I don't want any harm to come to you . . . Uncle.'

Matthew looked at her for a moment. 'Don't call me that, Phoebe. I am Matthew to you and always will be.'

'Why, it is what you are. We can not escape it now, can we?' Phoebe was glad that the spray of the sea camouflaged the moisture in her eyes.

'Not really. We are related by

marriage only, not by blood. When father married your grandmother, your mother was fourteen and I only six.' He stared at her across the boat pointedly then concentrated on manoeuvring the boat to the harbour of Ebton.

Phoebe didn't dare to think he was trying to tell her what she wanted to hear — that they were free, but was scared she had misunderstood and he was trying to distance himself from her. No more was said until they had run the small craft on to the beach north of the harbour. They ran for the cover of the dunes and then the marshes beyond, skirting the sand filled paths, hidden by the tall grasses and bulrushes.

'This land was used as saltings for many centuries. Salt has been a valuable commodity here for years.' Matthew was taking them to the outbuildings at the back of the town.

'Matthew, why do you still talk about God if your heart was never truly called to be a priest? Why didn't you run off

143

and join the army too?' Phoebe was surprised when Matthew turned around with a shocked expression on his face.

'You think my calling isn't genuine? Do you think I am merely dressing a part and performing like an actor when I deliver a sermon to the people?'

'You didn't want to be a priest, you said so. Your father forced you and besides, I haven't seen you preach.' Phoebe lifted a finger to his cheek. 'I don't doubt your honour or sincerity in whatever you do, Matthew.'

He wrapped his hand around her finger then kissed it gently. 'Thank you for that, but believe me, with what we have to do today, I would wish you far away from here. I pray you will be safe. I left the old church because I wanted to reach out to the poor, the used and the desolate.

'Initially, I thought I had to be a soldier to fight for what was just. The church taught me — or rather the bible taught me I was wrong.' Matthew continued along the path, which led behind the dunes to a clutch of fishermen's huts. Now, for both our sakes let us concentrate on the task before us, Phoebe. We must concentrate on what we need to do.'

'Why don't you just go to the garrison and have them all arrested — Reverend Hickworth, Seth Barton and anyone else you know about?' Phoebe asked.

'Because there is no point in stopping the workers, they can be replaced. We need to stop the man at the top who is the brains and money behind the organisation. He deals with more dangerous substances than silk, opium, baccy and brandy.' Matthew carefully opened one of the hut doors.

'Do you know who he is?' Phoebe asked wide-eyed.

'Yes, but without the proof, no-one will take me seriously.' Matthew rummaged around in a bag of clothes and found some sailors' slops. He cut about six inches off the cotton of the legs with his knife and told Phoebe to wear them held up by a string around the waist. She loved being in breeches. Matthew then pulled a wool hat on her head and a short jacket on her back with the sleeves turned up twice.

'I must look a sight,' Phoebe said and giggled.

'No, you look ... ' Matthew's manner abruptly turned, 'You should've stayed safe, warm and dry back at the house.' He shook his head as he pulled on a warm woollen coat, covering his pistols and cutlass.

'What, and let you get shot at?' Phoebe retorted.

Matthew looked down at her and smiled. 'My sincerest thanks for that. You followed your heart and did the Lord's work. Now firstly, I must get Mercy to safety then I shall finish my job.'

They were just about to leave the hut when they heard a dull thud against the wall like something thrown or crashing into it.

'Who else knows of this place,

Matthew?' Phoebe asked.

'This is one of the gang's safety hides. Here, anyone running from trouble finds fresh clothes, food and weapons. Sshh!' Matthew edged the door ajar with his pistol but something prevented it from moving far. He pushed harder and a voice groaned. Without hesitation he shoved with all his might against the door.

'Levi . . . help.' The voice was so feeble that Phoebe didn't recognise it until she saw her old enemy, Seth Barton, being carried in by Matthew. The rag that strapped his arm was covered in blood. It covered the stump of his right arm where once a hand held a cat that beat many a tired child. For all the hatred and loathing Phoebe had felt for the man, in her heart, she could only feel pity. He was pale, weak and sweating profusely.

'Seth, how did such a thing happen to you?' Matthew found a rag and unwrapped the man's wound. Phoebe watched him flinch as he saw and smelt the rotting wound. He lifted up a panel of wood from the makeshift wall and pulled out a skin of brandy. He poured it over the wound and wrapped it up, then gave Seth a good drink. Seth would not survive.

Seth stared intently at Matthew. He had no scarf over his face to hide his true identity. 'Matthew Fenton, the preacher man — you all along! You working for the preventative forces, eh?' Seth coughed loudly.

'Not quite. I want the proof that will name and shame the main man, Seth. He's the one who ordered this done to you.' Matthew was desperately trying to get Seth to help him catch the blackguard. Phoebe was crouching against the back wall of the hut in silence watching.

'No! It was Hickworth that done this because I went to his church. You know the rules. I broke them and he considered me a risk.' The man coughed violently and Phoebe could see the look of desperation and panic in

148

Matthew's face.

'Right, preacher man, I'll give you what you want and you give me what I need.' Seth, now a deathly grey colour gulped as Matthew nodded agreement.

'Your man keeps ledgers. He's greedy and arrogant. I heard how he keeps them in a box locked under his bed, in an old priest hole — names, dates and all. It would take an army to get in there as he lives in the part of the old house that was built like a keep.'

Matthew grinned. Phoebe thought that the information would be enough to complete Matthew's work.

'So what do you want of me, Seth?' Matthew asked.

'Your blessing. I've not been a good boy.' Seth tried to laugh and nearly choked. 'I wants forgiveness and absolution before I goes.'

Matthew took a deep breath. 'Tell me, Seth, who killed Sarah, the girl in the woods and why?'

'I shoved her down the well. She'd followed us and knew where we'd stashed the goods. She was wild, that one, lady or not. Now you gave your word, Priest.' Seth coughed.

'Seth Barton, it is not for man to judge your sin. I will ask for the Lord's forgiveness. Let us pray.'

Phoebe watched the man she then trusted, and later discovered to be her uncle, all-be-it through marriage, do the work he was truly meant to do. With sincerity and grace he prayed with, and blessed a man whom Phoebe had wished dead on many occasion. Yet she now felt extremely touched at the humility of the priest as Seth shuddered and left this world. He would never harm another soul on earth.

Quietly, Matthew had taken the rest of the clothes out and placed them underneath the hut. He then emptied the paraffin from an old oil lamp on to its floor and threw it underneath amidst the rags. Using his pistol shot, he started a fire. Matthew stepped back, prayed, then told Phoebe to run with him as fast as she could. They had to catch a king — not of the country, but the man known only to the locals as the *King of the smugglers* — a king who was about to be dethroned.

12

Thomas rushed back to the bedroom, or at least he thought he had but in the large strange house with more corridors and doors than he had ever seen in his life before, he was very lost. He flung open one door and discovered a room full of large portrait paintings.

He stared, amazed at the size of them, some almost from floor to ceiling were of a family group. The girl in one looked very like Phoebe. He saw Matthew and a man that must have been his older brother, William, dressed in a fine uniform. He too had a kindly face, Thomas thought.

Then he saw a smaller painting, which hung above a Wedgewood-style fireplace. A tear and a smile came to him at the same time, because there was the loving and tender face of their mother. She was some years younger, but her eyes and smile were just as he remembered.

Thomas was determined not to let Phoebe down, she was relying on him to help her and Matthew in their quest. He ran from door to door until he was greeted with a rather bemused Lord Fenton in his nightshift. He had risen and was stretching by the window when Thomas blustered in.

'My Lord,' Thomas bowed then without hesitation ran over to the rather amused figure as he pulled a robe around himself. 'We have things to do. We must go to Sunnington Hall to rescue Mercy, and then we must find Mother. She could be in an asylum and . . . '

'Young man. Please stop and take your breath. Now what is all this we must do, and where, pray, is your sister? In bed, I sincerely hope, but from your demeanour I am already doubting this.'

'Phoebe has gone with Matthew to save his life and I have clear instructions as to what we must do to save

Mercy and Mother.' Thomas held his grandfather's hand in his. 'They need us.'

Lord Fenton looked at Thomas's hand and then his own as if lost for words. For a moment Thomas thought he was about to rebuke him for his forwardness, but then he smiled broadly. 'I suspect that from this day forth my life will never be dull again.'

Thomas explained what had happened and what Phoebe had said to him.

Lord Fenton stood up and led him to the door. He pulled the servants' cord and Millie arrived. 'Millie, take Thomas to his room and find him some proper travelling clothes, then give him a hearty breakfast and bring him to me in the library in one hour. Have Philips fetch the buggy around to the front, ready to go.'

Thomas happily went with Millie. He found it extremely odd that the maid should think she was going to wash and dress him. Once suitably attired he sat down to a hearty breakfast of eggs, ham and freshly-baked bread. By the time he was reunited with his grandfather he was warm, full of both food and excitement.

'Where to first? Gumbel Beck, Grand . . . my Lord . . . ?' Thomas now did not know how he should address this man who was a stranger to him, despite their family ties.

'You may call me Grandfather, Thomas. After all, that is what I am and proud to be, too.' He led Thomas by the hand to Philips and the waiting buggy and lifted him up with the help of his man. Before they set off, he gave two letters to him and said, 'See to it that these are delivered, post haste!'

They set off down the drive. 'Where to, my Lord?' Philips asked.

'To Gumbel Workhouse as fast and safely as you can,' Lord Fenton replied.

'What about Mercy, Grandfather?'

'I've seen to that. I've ordered her to be detained by the dragoons on my behalf. She will be taken to the garrison and we shall collect her from there once we have finished our most important business. First things first. I fear that her situation will be far more commodious than that of your mother's if your theory is correct.

They travelled over the rickety old roads until they reached the new coach road. Then their journey was swifter and far more comfortable than it had been. A coach and horses overtook them at speed.

Thomas let out a shriek of delight and gripped his grandfather's arm. 'Look how fast they go!'

'Yes, and the poor horses, I feel for them. This country is going mad. Machines are replacing men and animals are worked like machines. Do you know how many drop dead in the harness and why? Because mankind is in such a hurry to get to wherever their destiny declares. The world is becoming a sad place, my dear Thomas.' He shook his head sombrely.

'Machines are good. They produce

more for less effort and should be used to help mankind, not replace them or be used to abuse them. If I were to run a mill I would treat the people like humans and the machines like machines. I'd also let black people work there fairly, too.'

'Well, well, Thomas you're a boy of great foresight.' His grandfather's face seemed to have lit up with a sort of hopeful expression. 'It looks as though my daughter has raised two fine children. I will see to it that you both have every opportunity in life to fulfil your dreams, Thomas. I may have let your mother down, but this I promise you. I shall not repeat my mistakes.'

'You thought you were doing what was best for her. She would not hate you for that. Everyone is wrong sometimes, even rich folk.' Thomas was surprised when his words of comfort made his grandfather laugh.

'Oh, my dear boy, especially rich folk.' Both of their smiles and banter stopped as they approached the gates of

Gumbel Beck Workhouse. Even from the outside the grey stone building looked run down and cold.

'You stay here, Thomas. I'll see to this.' His grandfather stepped down. He picked up his cane that had an ornate gold handle. It spoke instantly of position and money. He noted as Lord Fenton descended the step that a pistol was tucked inside his waistcoat.

He had not realised until he stepped away that a large man had been sitting on a tail seat behind them carrying a gun. He followed behind Lord Fenton as he knocked on the old doors.

Thomas ran up to him. 'I'll know if she's here, please let me come with you,' he begged.

'Thomas, you will see things that no child should.' Lord Fenton looked down on his desperate face with total compassion.

'I've already seen things I shouldn't,' Thomas answered honestly, as a small panel was opened in the huge door.

'What d'yer . . . Oh, 'scuse me yer

Lordship.' The harsh voice changed as soon as the wizened face saw Lord Fenton.

The door swung open, leading them into a slimy cobbled yard. It was the first time that Thomas had seen beyond the doors. What he saw made his stomach turn. Their lovely mother had been subjected to these bare stone walls, dripping with damp. Long empty rooms were filled with the poorest and weakest forms of humanity. The smell made Lord Fenton cover his nose with his neckerchief.

'Take me to Master Pelham immediately!' The old hag of a woman nodded and bowed in a fumbled curtsey as she scurried along a corridor with bolted doors on each side, to a room at the end.

'Just a minute your Lordship, Sir.' She backed into the room closing the door discreetly behind her. He looked at his man and instantly it was flung wide. Lord Fenton entered, followed swiftly by Thomas. His man stood in the doorway, a menacing figure that all but blocked it.

A short round man, warmly dressed, pulled a serviette from his collar, placed a pewter plate down on the table by the warm fire and smiled. Thomas saw the smile on his lips but looked at the anger visible in his eyes. He had been caught stuffing his face in warmth and comfort, lazing by his fire, whilst his charges were near to starving or dying of the cold. 'What, pray, can I do for you, my Lord?'

'Florence Elgie née Fenton. She was brought here. Where is she?' The Lord's question had shocked the fat man. He shook his head, though, and pulled a big ledger from a shelf.

'The name does not sound familiar to me. Perhaps she was taken to another workhouse over Ashondale way, maybe.' The man fumbled through the pages.

Thomas jumped, as did Master Pelham when Lord Fenton crashed his stick down on the table knocking it over. Instantly his man slammed the door shut and the old hag crumpled into a heap against the wall. His grandfather turned and pointed his stick at her. 'Perhaps you know?'

She whimpered pathetically looking from the fat man to Thomas's grandfather.

'I . . . I . . . '

'She knows nothing of what goes on here,' the fat man said and stared at her.

Lord Fenton nodded to his man, who pointed the large gun at the hag's head. 'Mr Atkins paid to 'ave her put into the asylum. She's alive but locked up, like. He said as once his business is done, he'll take her home. When she's better, like.'

He stared at Master Pelham. 'You, Sir, will shortly join the inmates here.' He turned to his man and ordered, 'Stay here and guard them. I'll send Philips for you when I've located my Florence.'

Thomas and Lord Fenton left,

leaving the gate unattended and wide open. It took twenty more long minutes to drive over to the asylum.

'Thomas I think you really ought to stay here . . . '

'No, she'll need me!' Thomas answered, his voice trembling.

The asylum was marginally better run than the workhouse. Wasted humanity, often chained in one large hall, was displayed with a viewing gallery in order that those so-called normal members of society that wanted to, could stand and gawk at the poor demented creatures. The asylum guards escorted them to the office. This time Lord Fenton had to adopt a new tactic.

'Sir, I'll come straight to the point. You have Florence Elgie here. She is not mad and is being held here against her wishes by Atkins.'

The tall sombrely-dressed man stared quizzically back at Lord Fenton and raised an eyebrow.

'I am her father. I want her returned

to me. How much is he paying you to keep her here?'

'My dear Sir, what you are inferring is that I have acted both illegally and immorally,' the man said coolly. 'I have a statement signed by our Doctor Goodbody to say she has sadly succumbed to a poor state of mind, known as lunacy.'

'I am sure you have, and I am here to purchase such a statement to say she has recovered. Do we understand ourselves clearly? I can assure you that Mr Atkins will not be returning for her, ever!'

'Do I have the word of a gentleman on that?' the man asked.

'Absolutely,' Lord Fenton answered.

He rang a bell and instantly the man who had shown them into the office opened the door. 'Collins, bring number two, three, five to this office.'

Thomas wanted to run after him. He could hardly contain his excitement at the thought of seeing his mother again.

Lord Fenton and the gaunt man muttered between themselves and exchanged signed pieces of paper.

When the door opened ten minutes later a figure was pushed through that bore some resemblance to the woman Thomas had called his mother. She was dressed plainly and cleanly but was so thin. Where once bright eyes had shone, deep pools looked at the people in the room as if unable to take in what was before her.

Thomas ran to her and hugged her so tightly that she gasped. 'Mother!'

The stunned woman looked down and Thomas saw an amazing sight. The dull eyes filled with tears, the pinched lips broadened and smiled, and the pale cheeks flushed. 'Didy.' One word swelled with enough love and emotion to communicate everything she felt and wanted to say.

Lord Fenton put a kindly hand on his daughter's back. 'Come Flo, you're coming home.'

'Where's Phoebe?' Florence asked

shakily as if scared of the answer.

'She's all right, Mother, she's looking after Matthew.' Thomas led the stunned and happy woman by the hand back to the buggy.

13

Phoebe ran after Matthew. They didn't stop until both of them had reached the cover of a wooded ravine south of Ebton, climbing through the trees and up the steep bank until they came to the edge of a field. There, Matthew lay down in the shelter of the long grass. Phoebe collapsed alongside him.

She did not really want to think too much about the frightening and dangerous task ahead of them. She watched as Matthew checked his pistols, and then drank from a small silver flask. 'Here drink some of this, but just a little.'

Phoebe took the flask gratefully. She had never held something so valuable and fine before. It even had an engraving of a family crest on it, below which some words were engraved. 'What does that say?' she asked.

'Be true to God, your family and yourself. It is the Fenton family motto. One I have always been proud of.'

Phoebe drank happily from the family flask — her family. The liquid reached the back of her throat and she coughed. 'Matthew, whose bed is the box under? Unless you know who 'he' is, we're no better off, are we?' Phoebe passed the flask back to Matthew.

'Atkins! Otherwise known as the Lord of Sunnington Hall — a forty thousand acre estate — traitor, drug dealer and murderer to boot, but at last he shall pay for his crimes. We shall have the proof and nobody will be able to protect him from the penalty for treason.' Matthew closed his eyes and rested.

'Drug dealer?' Phoebe repeated.

'Opium, for the drug dens of London.'

'I thought it was a medicine like laudanum.' Phoebe had known a woman who took the latter frequently to sleep.

'Phoebe, when a drug is taken because it makes you feel better when your spirits are low, the danger is that, when you don't take it, you feel worse then ever. It's called being addicted and bad men, greedy men like Atkins, profit as the addicts sink into a living hell. Don't ever take things like that for pleasure. The benefits are always short lived.'

'I won't, but Matthew, there is something I can't understand,' Phoebe said as she watched her uncle, whilst trying to get used to the idea that she suddenly had a family, and one of standing at that. 'How could you forgive Seth Barton for murdering your fiancée's sister, Sarah?' Phoebe watched Matthew's face for his reaction.

Matthew opened his eyes and looked at Phoebe. 'As a man of God I should be able to, but I didn't actually say I had, Phoebe. I asked God to. It is for him to judge the man. He is much greater than I.'

'Have you, though?' Phoebe persisted.

'I'm struggling with it. I'm human, Phoebe. It is God who is divine.' Matthew closed his eyes again and lay back. 'And I never said that Mercy was my fiancée.'

'Oh, I presumed . . . '

'Don't.'

'Was she?' Phoebe persisted.

'Your instincts played you false this time, we were merely good friends.'

'Who gave you that scar on your neck?' Phoebe changed the subject and laughed as Matthew self-consciously pulled his scarf up a little.

'It was William, when we were playing soldiers — he nearly cut my throat accidentally.'

'I thought the eldest son was supposed to stay and see to the estate, the second became a soldier and the third a priest,' Phoebe said. She wanted to impress Matthew with her know-ledge about the ways of the rich.

'My father owns a manor house and has plenty of money, but not invested in land to oversee. Besides, he has had only two sons. He wanted William to be more worldly before inheriting, and myself to be a more settled person.' Matthew was starting to become restless.

'Were you a bit on the wild side then?' Phoebe wanted to stay and talk all day. She had a family now and she was thirsty to know more about them.

Matthew glanced at her, but made no attempt to answer her question.

'Matthew . . . I . . . we . . . ' Phoebe knew what was in her heart to say, but her words failed her.

He looked at Phoebe. 'I like you, but I have not known either of you very long. What if I did want to get to know you more closely?'

'Do you only look upon me as my mother's daughter, Matthew?'

'No, Phoebe. Believe me when I tell you I see you very much as the woman — the person you are.'

Phoebe looked up at the man who had taken her life by storm, rescued them, restored them to their true family and felt nothing but love and respect for him. 'I think you could love us both.'

'We have too much to do now to worry over what may happen tomorrow.'

'Have I upset you?' Phoebe thought Matthew was angry with her, because he moved away so quickly.

'No, you haven't upset me. It's just that intelligence officers are supposed to ask the questions. We don't like being interrogated, it makes us uneasy. Also, Phoebe, now is not the time to relax too much and be comfortable. We have two villains to outwit and a lady to rescue first.'

'Is that what they call you, an Intelligence Officer?' Phoebe asked excitedly. 'Have you been to France then?'

'Yes and yes. Now can I ask you to be quiet because we need to creep up to the house unnoticed?' Matthew continued.

'Don't worry about Mercy. I asked

Thomas to get Lord Fenton to rescue her,' Phoebe said proudly and was amazed when Matthew spun around.

'You did what?' Matthew's face paled.

'They've gone for Mother, too. I thought you'd be pleased.' Phoebe stopped. She was very unsure what Matthew was going to do.

'Phoebe, I needed Mercy in the house to get into the hall to gain access to Atkins' room.' He ran his hand through his hair.

'Surely her safety is more important to you than Atkins and his drugs?' Phoebe said defensively.

'Phoebe, listen to me carefully. This is more important than you, Sarah, me or even, God help me, Mercy. The man is a spy. He sells and buys goods from the French, but worse, he sells secrets — state secrets to men who work for Napoleon Bonaparte himself. If he and people like him aren't stopped we might lose this war. Our land, our lives will not be ours any more.'

Phoebe and Matthew moved as near to the Hall as they could, then stayed within the cover of the trees out of sight until darkness fell. In the late afternoon they saw a group of dragoons arrive. The Lieutenant entered and, after several moments, left escorting Mercy Bright.

'Father has followed your instructions, Phoebe. Mercy is safely out of the way. She will be safe now.' Matthew was gripping the handle of his pistol firmly.

'Why don't we ask them to search his Lordship's room? That way they'd know what he was doing and could lock him up straightaway,' Phoebe asked.

'I wish it was that simple. Someone in the dragoons is in his pay. It could be the Lieutenant.' Matthew watched the troops leave, taking Mercy with them down the long drive.

'It's not him. He came to the cottage with Hickworth, but he wasn't friendly with him because he even accused Hickworth of being jealous of you.' Phoebe was pleased she could give

Matthew some useful information.

'Jealous of me? Why so?' Matthew looked at her genuinely surprised.

'Because more people listen to you than him and his miserable sermons.' Phoebe wrinkled her nose.

Matthew laughed. 'Well, he hardly speaks from the heart, does he?'

The moment darkness fell, the two crept around the back of the Hall. They slipped in via the scullery and, as the servants tended his Lordship's guests in the large dining room, Phoebe and Matthew made their way up one of the servants' staircases to the wing of the bedrooms. They faced a long corridor of doors.

'Which one is his?' Phoebe asked.

'The grandest, or largest. We shall know.' Matthew and Phoebe tiptoed as quickly as they could to a door that had a family crest above it. Matthew nodded and tucked Phoebe behind him. 'Stay here and keep lookout for me.'

Matthew had not taken two steps

when he heard a snore. Phoebe peeped around the doorway and saw a figure lying in bed, deeply asleep. An empty bottle and glass stood on a bedside table. His Lordship was in a drunken stupor. Matthew kept his pistol trained on the figure and looked under the bed. He was a big man and could not easily slide underneath it.

Phoebe had been peering round the doorway and not watching the corridor. Matthew saw her and waved at her to come in. He pointed to the floor and Phoebe swiftly disappeared underneath the bed. Matthew trained his gun on the heaving figure as it moved uneasily, then sat bolt upright, staring straight at him.

'What in damnation are you doing here?' Phoebe heard the man shout.

'One more word out of you and the family line will move on a generation.' Matthew lowered his voice but sounded totally convincing. Phoebe fumbled around in the dark until she found the hiding place as Seth Barton had described. As quietly as she could she lifted a piece of wood and retrieved a small book tied in a leather cloth.

'Go on, shoot me. Have the whole household down here before you reach the door.' Atkins laughed and reached for the servants' bell.

Phoebe poked her head out from under the bed just in time to see Matthew hit the man across the head with the handle of the pistol. Matthew wasted no time. He picked up a silk neckerchief that was thrown over a chair and tied the man's hands behind his back. He tied his own scarf as a gag around Atkins' mouth and then hurried Phoebe out of the room.

All was going well. They slipped out the way they had entered. 'Phoebe, we'll cut through the churchyard and use the tunnel in the stables to get back to Stangcliffe.'

Phoebe followed Matthew as he ran past a large marble tomb. She was feeling decidedly nervous when, all of a sudden, a black figure blocked their path. For one awful moment Phoebe thought the devil himself had appeared but then the figure spoke in a familiar, menacing voice.

'Going somewhere in a hurry, Fenton?' He drew a pistol from under his coat.

'Hickworth, get out of my way.'

'Big words for a little man — that is what you are. This operation is too big for the likes of an interfering do-gooder. You should have stayed on your donkey and kept company with the destitute and poor.'

'Get out of my way before I make you,' Matthew repeated.

Hickworth aimed the gun at Matthew's head. 'Goodbye, Fenton, go meet your maker.' Before he had a chance to fire the shot another gun fired and the Reverend Hickworth fell down to his knees then landed flat on his face in front of a gravestone.

Phoebe ran over to Matthew. 'You killed him.'

Lights went on in the house. Torches were lighting up the grounds — the alarm had been raised.

'Quickly, Phoebe, there is no time to lose!' They jumped over Hickworth's body. He had been so certain of his own power that he had not seen that Matthew already had a pistol loaded ready, and in his hand. Phoebe glanced at the tombstone and saw the name, *Sarah Bright* inscribed on it.

Once in the stables, Matthew lifted the trapdoor and down the tunnel they ran as servants chased across the yard. The tunnel was pitch black but Matthew knew the way so well he was able to lead Phoebe safely to the cottage. They pushed the door open wide and were greeted by the captain of the dragoons.

'So it is true. There is a tunnel from the Hall to the bay. How convenient,' the officer said, and held a hand out to welcome Matthew.

Matthew nodded. 'It should be sealed up from now on, I think,' Matthew answered and looked around uncertainly.

'You've something which will be of great interest to me, I hope, sir!' He continued to hold out his hand, this time to receive the book.

Matthew hesitated and looked to the doorway. Footsteps were coming nearer, and then two servants alighted from the tunnel. The sergeant of the dragoons appeared at the doorway. He sneered as he saw Matthew, then stumbled in as a soldier pushed him from behind.

'This is the traitor at the garrison, Fenton, not I.' The Captain told the servants to wait at the inn. He ordered his men into the cottage and had them file, with torches, up the tunnel to the Hall. Half went into the tunnel whilst the others were told to block off the roads. 'His Lordship must not escape!' The order was given.

Matthew produced the book and handed it over to the Captain of the guard. 'Well done, Fenton!'

Matthew allowed the man a quick look at it, and then took it back. 'I need

that for my superior at Horseguards.'
Phoebe thought Matthew looked tired.
She had never given any thought to the
fact that he had been under a lot of
pressure to catch the spy.

The Captain nodded his agreement.
'The country is indebted to you
— both!' He smiled at Phoebe. 'Now I
understand your father,' he looked at
Matthew, 'and your brother and mother
are awaiting your presence at the
Manor house.'

He looked at Phoebe and she
repeated, 'They found Mother?'

'Yes, young lady. I'll have an escort
take you both there, forthwith. Fenton,
come to the garrison tomorrow and I'll
have men ready to accompany you to
London.'

They were glad to be taken back to
Lord Fenton. Phoebe ran straight into
her mother's arms. No words were
spoken and no words were needed.
They had all come home.

After a late supper, their grandfather
stood and toasted his family. 'And now,

my lovelies, I have received one more piece of news today that I hope will please you. With Matthew's contacts we have located the whereabouts of your father.'

Thomas, Phoebe and Florence stood up. 'Where is he — Father?' Phoebe asked.

'He took a bad wound and was left for dead. Apparently he recovered enough, with the help of some resistance fighters, to be taken to the local port. I have sent funds for his return to us. He is in no state to fight any more as he has lost some muscle use in his arm, I understand, but we should expect his arrival here within the month.'

* * *

Phoebe talked to her mother until the woman fell asleep out of emotional exhaustion. Then Phoebe left her clean and safe in her bed and ventured down the sweeping staircase. She saw that there was a flickering light in the study and quietly entered. Matthew sat at the desk, his head resting in his hands.

'I hoped you would come,' he said and strode over to meet her.

'Your job is done, Matthew.' Phoebe smiled at him as he held her hands and led her to the sofa by the fire.

'This one, yes, but there will be others and that is my dilemma.' He stroked her cheek gently.

'You feel for me as I do for you, Matthew. Are you scared that your father or sister will reject us?'

He placed his arm around her and drew her to him. 'No, my love, I fear for you. For the life I offer is not routine or stable. Both my positions mean I travel in dangerous places and times. That is nothing to offer a young lady.'

'Why don't you let the young lady in question make up her own mind as to the worthiness of your offer when you make it.' Phoebe raised an eyebrow at him and he immediately dropped to one knee by her side.

'Phoebe Elgie, I offer you a tumultuous future, an uncertain path and all my heart and soul. Will you be my wife and soulmate?'

'Matthew Fenton, I only have my heart and soul to offer, but I freely give them to you and accept yours.'

They hugged each other as though they would never let go again, unaware that Lord Fenton watched them from the doorway with a tear in his eye and a truly happy heart.

THE END

FORSAKING ALL OTHERS

Jane Carrick

Dr Shirley Baxter, after several inexcusable mistakes, leaves her London hospital to look after her sick grandfather in Inverdorran. However, with the help of locum Dr Andrews, he soon recovers. Shirley meets and falls in love with Neil Fraser who is working hard to build a local leisure centre. But Neil's plans are beset with problems, and after he suffers a breakdown, Shirley finds her medical training is once again in demand.

FORBIDDEN LOVE

Zelma Falkiner

By the time Lyndal Frazer learns the identity of the stranger who rescued her and her sheepdog, Rowdy, from drowning, it is too late. She has fallen half in love with a sworn enemy of her ailing father. Torn between growing attraction and duty, Lyndal chooses family loyalty. But Hugh Trevellyn has made up his mind, too; a bitter feud will not be allowed to come between them.